The Reunion

Here I was, in foreign parts right enough, and alone, going through Customs and Immigration where the man seemed to think I was up to no good and questioned me persistently about my motives for coming.

I scanned the faces of the people who were crammed against the barrier anxiously searching for arriving friends and relatives. Every second someone got up on their toes, waved and shouted, 'Hi!' There seemed to be no sign at all of Phil. Then I heard a voice calling 'Maggie!'

MAGGIE

Book 4

The Reunion

Joan Lingard

Beaver Books

A Beaver Book

Published by Arrow Books Limited
62–5 Chandos Place, London WC2N 4NW

An imprint of Century Hutchinson Ltd

London Melbourne Sydney Auckland
Johannesburg and agencies throughout
the world

First published by Hamish Hamilton 1977

Beaver edition 1981
Fourth impression 1987

Text © Joan Lingard 1977

Printed and bound in Great Britain by
Cox & Wyman Ltd, Reading

ISBN 0 09 951260 2

For my Canadian nieces
Andra, Inta, Mara and Benita

Chapter 1

We made sure our seat belts were securely fastened and seats in the upright position; we were ready for take-off. I could hardly believe that the moment had come, and now that it had I wasn't sure I wanted it.

I was taking off on a jet plane, a jumbo jet at that, for North America. There was an air of unreality about everything and I felt as if I was sitting in a cinema waiting for the show to begin. Which it would, later. We were going to be entertained by Liza Minnelli. Somewhere down below stood my father in his navy-blue Sunday suit and my Uncle Tam, and in the car park their van, with McKinley and Campbell, Sanitary Engineers, written on the side, was parked. I wanted to jump out and run and find my father and uncle and get into the van and drive back to Glasgow where my mother and Aunt Jessie would be sitting in the front shop consoling themselves with cups of tea and wondering if I was there yet. There being Toronto. Neither of them have much sense of time or place. Jump out now? I looked over at the window and saw clouds. McKinley, you've had it! I was on my way whether I liked it or not. The take-off had been so smooth I hadn't registered the actual moment of leaving the ground.

'Typical of you, Maggie,' my old English teacher Mr Scott would have said, if he'd been sitting in the seat beside me, and I only wished he was, along with his wife and kids, and my father and mother and brother and sister and aunt and uncle and cousins. I would have been fine if they had all been there too. Mr Scott would have said that with anything new I started raising panic stations all around me until eventually I calmed down, subsided and began to take notice of the situation itself and got interested. I was planning to be a social anthropologist which meant that I couldn't sit in Glasgow or even Scotland all my life.

Not that I wanted to – the world outside looked far too interesting and I was dying to cross the Kalahari, sail down the Nile or even walk up the Champs-Elysées – but getting away was as sure as heck going to be a right carry on every time. My mother would be packing laxative tablets, Aunt Jessie telling me to be sure and mind to put on plenty of cold cream so that I wouldn't get burnt, my dad pacing the sitting-room floor flicking cigarette ash on the carpet, and I would be hollering loudly about the things I'd meant to do and hadn't, maddening them all.

As we went up and up, and my ears began to pop ever so slightly, I wondered if I was suffering from that business known as the cutting of the cord. I've not been the type to be tied to my mother's apron strings, mind you; far from it! Since I was five years old and got away to the school my mother has been trying to catch hold of *my* heels. And I hadn't leant on her or expected her to do things for me; if anything, it had been the other way round the last few years. But that was neither here nor there, the leaning or being leant on: it was the parting that mattered. I hated goodbyes, was bad at them.

Ten minutes before we'd had to go through Customs I'd turned to my father, who was taking a wee dram in the airport bar to steady his nerves, and said, 'I'm not going, Dad. I've changed my mind.' 'Not going? Are you daft or

8

something?' 'Maybe. But I'm still not going.' 'You're going, my lass, after all this fuss and bother.' In the beginning I'd had to fight every inch of the way for them to agree that I could go. 'I've gone off the idea,' I told him. He told me, 'You get on that plane, Maggie McKinley, and see you enjoy yourself!' 'You'll be all right once you're there,' Uncle Tam had added.

Well, I wasn't there yet, and I wasn't all right. It was the very first time I'd flown. And it was the first time I had ever been out of Scotland. Once I had almost gone to Italy on a skiing trip (not really my scene, the skiing; I fancied Italy), but I sprained my ankle on the way to the meeting point. Another typical McKinley move, some people would tell you. The plane gave a lurch, almost throwing me on to the lap of the woman beside me, and I said, 'Is it all right? The plane, I mean.' I glanced warily towards the window half expecting to see that one wing had fallen off. 'It's fine,' the woman said with a North American nasal twang. 'Just an air pocket.' I'd been practising the North American accent at home, making my mother and aunt kill themselves laughing, as they termed it. My companion didn't seem too keen to engage in conversation; she opened a magazine and began to read the advice column. 'How to Cope with Halitosis.' I eyed her, wondering if she had it. She didn't seem at all bothered to be thirty thousand feet or so above the ground. To me it was one of the inexplicable miracles of science.

We were actually in the clouds. They floated slowly past like pale milky skeins of wool. I gulped. I would have been perfectly all right if only . . . if only my granny hadn't died ten days before. That was really what was the matter with me. Everything else was a detail, unimportant compared to that one fact. She had died suddenly, of heart failure in her sleep, in her little flat up in Inverness-shire. We had had a very special thing going between us, she and I, and every time I'd left her I had thought that perhaps that would be the last time I'd wave and see her old bent figure in its flowered wrap-around overall and men's laced-up boots waving back to me.

'Are you okay, kid? Are you feeling sick or something?'

I gulped, said no, I was fine. The woman went back to halitosis and I to the clouds. Presumably the sea was beneath us now, the Atlantic Ocean, sparkling in sunshine, though I couldn't see it. The Scottish coast must already be behind us.

My granny was eighty-five years old when she died, and as everyone said, spouting clichés as they always do at times like that, she'd had a good life and no one can live for ever. Well, of course I *knew* that, but it didn't make any difference. I wouldn't say I'd expected her to live for ever but I'd kind of hoped that even if eternity wasn't a possibility, something close to it was. I needed her. She was a part of my life and then, suddenly, she wasn't, not any more.

That day, as I was coming home from the bookbinders where I had been working for the past eight months, I wasn't thinking about death, either hers or anyone else's. Far from it. I was thinking how marvellous the world was, how bright the early summer sunshine, how nice Glasgow looked, and how much I was looking forward to going to Canada, a whole new country, for me, and to meeting Phil Ross again. And I thought, 'Only one more week to go at the bookbinders, thank goodness!' I gave a little skip. They had been long, boring, tedious months, but it had all been worthwhile for I had in my bank the money for the summer as well as some to take me on to university in the autumn.

When I rounded the last corner home I saw that our shop was closed and padlocked. It was early for them to have closed up, for usually my father and uncle were dithering around until quite late in the evening but, even then, it didn't occur to me that something might be wrong. I went upstairs whistling, calling out, 'Anyone in? Or are you all deid?' There was not a sound in the house.

I opened the sitting-room door. Sitting around in a semi-circle were my mother and father, sister Jean and brother Sandy, Uncle Tam and Aunt Jessie. They had faces as long as your arm on them. I was used to them sitting about with long faces and so didn't suspect anything too serious. Five pounds stolen from the till was enough to produce depression in my family. They always over-reacted. Like me? Yes, like me.

'What's up now?' I asked brightly. I felt in good form: the breath of summer sunshine was still in my lungs. It was the last time I felt in good form for some time.

My father got up and came towards me. His eyes looked kind of haunted and for the first time I began to feel alarm.

'What is it, Dad?'

He put his hand on my shoulder; he seemed to want to speak. His Adam's apple went up and down. I watched it, mesmerised.

'Maggie,' said my mother, also getting up, 'this is going to be a bit of a shock for you, lass—'

I stared at them. I knew now, I sensed it.

'Something's happened to Gran?' My father nodded. I went on, 'Is she dead?' Again, he nodded.

'Now you mustn't take on too much, Maggie,' said my mother, putting her arm round me. 'She was eighty-five, you know.'

'That's a right good age,' said Uncle Tam. 'If we could all live as long we'd be doing all right.'

'She had a good death,' said my father, speaking in a slow, stunned voice. 'Heart attack. Over in minutes, they said.'

11

'It's a good way to go,' said Aunt Jessie. 'If you have to go, that is.'

'No suffering,' said my father.

'She wouldn't want you to grieve, Maggie,' said my mother.

'How do you know?' I cried. 'You hardly knew her. None of you did, not really. I knew her better than any of you.'

Perhaps it was not strictly true, for she had been the mother of my father, whereas she had only been my grandmother, but I felt it to be true. Had I not gone up there to Inverness-shire every chance I could to see her, whereas they had gone but seldom, and only under protest? We had been close, she and I, and I had been able to tell her things that I had never been able to tell anyone else.

Swiftly I turned, and ran from the room, down the stairs and back out into the streets of Glasgow.

'Anything to drink?'

I started, looking up, to see the air stewardess bending over me enquiringly. Beside her in the alleyway she had a trolley of drinks.

'Oh, orange juice, please.'

I took the orange juice and pulled down the little tray from the back of the seat in front of me. Apparently we could unfasten our seat belts and lower our seats now, if we wished. I decided to keep my seat belt fastened, just to make sure.

I sipped my orange juice and the woman beside me closed her magazine to drink her vodka and orange and engage me in conversation. She asked if it was the first time I had flown and I confessed that it was, knowing full well that it must be written all over me. She patted my knee and told me that there was nothing to worry about, these planes were marvellous and they took real good care of you. She talked to me until dinner was served.

We had smoked salmon and asparagus, chicken in tomato sauce with broccoli and croquette potatoes, apple pie and cream and a roll with cheese, and a cup of coffee. I thought I would burst by the time I'd got through the lot. My companion said contentedly that they fed you all the way across the Atlantic, it helped take your mind off the flying. The stewardesses came to clear away the debris and we settled back to watch the film.

I found the earphones dug into my ears and I had to squint sideways to catch a glimpse of Liza Minnelli, so what with that, and all the food inside me, I soon drifted off into sleep.

We had gone up to Inverness-shire in the van for the funeral. It was kind of cramped and uncomfortable but nobody was caring about things like that compared with what we had to face ahead. It was another bright sunny June day, just like the one on which she'd died. The mountains were glistening and the glens beautiful, so beautiful that they brought a catch to the back of my throat. How she would have loved to have leant on her gatepost and gazed at the changing light on the hills! Her eyes had always been turned towards those hills. It was as if she was a part of them, and they of her.

She was buried in the old churchyard not far from where she'd spent her life, the place where her husband had been buried, and her forebears before her. Our forebears. There were a lot of people there apart from us, the McKinleys; there were people from the farms and crofts round about, people from the small town where she had lived for the last two or three years, and also, the Frasers from Edinburgh.

I hadn't thought about the Frasers coming to the

funeral. Since I'd heard that my granny had died I hadn't thought of anything else but her, remembering times we'd spent together, things we'd talked about, and things we'd laughed over. And so when I saw Mr and Mrs Fraser and their son James coming into the church, I was startled.

James and I had gone steady for a year and he had asked me to marry him at the end of it. It was the first time in months that we had seen one another and both of us looked up from our hymn books, embarrassed, blushing. I looked away first.

'It was awful nice of you to come,' said my mother as she shook hands with Mrs Fraser after the burial service. I knew my family greatly regretted my rejection of James.

'We wouldn't have dreamt of not coming,' said Mrs Fraser. 'We were exceedingly fond of Mrs McKinley. She was a marvellous woman.'

I moved a few yards away from them and stood at the edge of the graveyard, looking back towards the hills, listening to the distant lowing of the cows and bleating of the sheep. This was a peaceful spot and I knew that it was where she would have wanted to have been laid to rest for the last time.

James came up behind me and I turned a little and nodded, just to recognise his presence. He began to say that he was sorry and I told him it was all right, even though it obviously was not.

He cleared his throat. 'I know she meant a lot to you, Maggie.' He could not go on, not knowing what to say, and I didn't want him to say anything more, but at that moment I was grateful to have him standing there beside me, for I knew that he did understand, and appreciated fully what she had been to me. I doubted if anyone else in my family knew it as well. He had seen us together more than anyone else had.

'It's nice to be in the glen again, isn't it?' he said.

It was true, even though the circumstances were sad. We had spent many happy days together in this glen, he and I. And in the end I knew I hurt him a lot. But I had no other choice, for I had not wanted to marry. So I stood there staring at the hills, feeling the warmth of the sun on my back and suffering a confusion of painful emotions.

We walked a little way, leaving the churchyard for the narrow winding road on which we had often strolled together, hand in hand. Our hands did not touch now. I asked him how he was getting on at university. He was just finishing his first year in medicine. We talked rather formally, he telling me about the university and I telling him about the bookbinders.

'But you'll be coming to Edinburgh in October?' he said.

Indeed I would, and I knew the thought was running through his mind that perhaps then we would see one another again. And at that moment I felt that perhaps we might, it was not impossible. I asked after his sister Catriona and her husband Alexander, and he shrugged, saying they seemed to be all right. I asked James to tell her that I was asking for her, and he said that he would. It seemed incredible that we were having this stilted, formal conversation when once we had been so close. It pained me that so much was lost. I said that we had better turn back and join the others. We were going to have a meal in the hotel and my father had asked the Frasers to join us.

It was a funny meal: my father and Uncle Tam drank too much, I ate nothing at all, and Mrs Fraser talked most of the time to my Aunt Jessie who kept nodding in agreement and eyeing James slyly.

'I'm going for a walk,' I said abruptly, and got up.

'Can I come with you?' asked James.

'Away you go, the two of you,' said my mother.

'The fresh air'll do you good.'

I jerked awake to see the last two minutes of Liza Minnelli. She was mouthing away vigorously, weaving her head about a lot. My earplug had slipped. Yawning, feeling crumpled and overfed, I tried to straighten myself out. I was longing now to get out on the ground and stretch my legs and arms wide.

'Great film,' said the woman beside me.

The stewardesses were bringing the trolley round with the afternoon tea. I couldn't believe that we were expected to start eating again so soon. My companion chuckled, saying that she'd told me they fed you well, hadn't she? I gazed at the scones and sandwiches in front of me but was unable to eat a crumb. I drank a cup of tea and left it at that. We would soon be over Toronto.

Toronto. I had thought that during the flight I would be thinking of nothing else, and about Phil Ross. And instead of which I had been thinking about my granny and James Fraser. Strange perverse creature that you are, McKinley!

I had met Phil Ross the summer before when I was hostelling in Easter Ross with James. We had only known one another for about a week but we had got on extraordinarily well right from the start. We 'clicked' (another of my mother's words), and when he went back to Canada we wrote to one another regularly. In one letter he suggested that I might like to come over and work in Canada for the summer and, if so, he would arrange a job for me. It had seemed like a fantastic idea, a chance to earn money in a new country, and to meet him again.

All through those long months at the bookbinders, whilst I had been stitching pages together, clocking in in the morning, checking out at night, doing a job that required little thinking on my part but was simply a routine manual expertise which I soon acquired, I had found that I had a lot of time to think. And whilst I was sitting there I had thought about Phil Ross, remembering his dark eyes and the way he had laughed and the way he had looked at me. I remembered tramping up Strathcarron with him, to Greenyards and Glencalvie, I remembered him giving me the stones he had collected over on the west coast. It helped the hours to pass. And now, in only an hour or so, I would see him again. And now that the time was so close I could hardly remember what he looked like. I felt that I was going to meet a stranger. After all, I *had* only known him for one week. And then I reminded myself that I was going to Canada, not only to see him, but to experience a new country, and to work. I had a job all lined up looking after three children aged between three and ten years at a good wage with bed and board thrown in. The woman had written me a letter asking me to send my particulars and a photograph, which I did, choosing a flattering likeness of myself, needless to say; and that had been that. A further brief letter had confirmed my appointment.

We were being told to fasten our seat belts again, we were getting ready to land at Toronto airport. My throat was dry, at the prospect of landing and at the reunion with Phil Ross. Deliberately, I turned my thoughts away from both.

James and I walked along the street of the little town towards the building where my granny had had a flat. We walked side by side, saying very little. We went inside and called on one or two of the old folk who had been Granny's friends. Old Mr Farquharson looked older and more mournful than ever, owing to my granny's death, I suspected. He mumbled on about how he thought he had little time left himself, his call would come next, and we tried to cheer him up by saying that he looked hale and hearty and I offered to do his washing or scrub his kitchen floor. In the past I had often done those chores for him but today he was not even up to accepting them, or trying to get me to make him a pot of soup. We left him sitting by his empty fireside muttering to himself.

Mrs Clark upstairs was a little less mournful, though she sighed a lot as she patted up her blue-rinsed hair. She would miss my granny dearly; they had spent many a winter evening together. Then she reached over and touched my hand and said that she knew how much I must miss her. There were tears in her eyes, and, yes, in mine too.

From there James and I made our way from the town along the road towards the glen. Only an occasional car passed us and we met no one walking. The birds were singing lustily in the trees overhead. I felt easier here than I had in Glasgow, I still felt as if my granny must be around somewhere and I kept thinking that when I got back I would tell her what I'd seen and done.

'It's a bit like old times,' said James. 'Except—'

'Yes, except.'

'I've missed you all those months, you know.'

I had missed him too, there was no doubt about that, but I had not known whether to say it or not. It was the truth, but might mislead him. I decided to say nothing. Then I felt his hand sliding into mine and taking it. He squeezed my fingers tight.

'I'd like to – well, start seeing you again, Maggie.'

Still I did not know what to say. I liked the feel of his hand around mine, it was warm and comforting, and I felt in need of warmth and comfort. I had felt cold right through to the marrow of my bones since the day I'd returned from the bookbinders' to find my world had changed. 'Jamie's a nice lad,' I could imagine my granny saying. She had been very fond of him and he of her. I turned to him.

'I've missed you too.'

'Have you really, Maggie? Honestly?'

He stopped and put his arms around me, then bent his head and kissed me.

We were about to land at Toronto, the captain was informing us. Toronto, Canada. A new country and a new continent. Were we really there?

We landed as smoothly as we'd taken off. Everyone was unfastening their safety belts and reaching up to the lockers overhead for their bits of hand luggage. I had numerous bits in paper carriers, things that I'd remembered at the last minute that wouldn't go into my suitcases. The plane was alive now with people stretching and yawning. We had come such a long way in a short time that I didn't know if I felt up to it yet: the arrival. 'You'd never feel up to it,' I could imagine Mr Scott telling me, 'so get on with it!'

'Somebody meeting you, dear?' asked the woman beside me.

Yes, I told her, a friend was meeting me.

A friend? 'Who is this laddie you're going away over there to see?' my mother had wanted to know when I had first told her of the plan. I was not going to see *him*, I told her; I was going to explore a new way of life, observe a different culture at close hand, broaden my horizons, earn money. I went on talking for so long that my mother had no chance to persist in her questions about Phil Ross. I wouldn't have known the answers if she had. I seemed to know too few answers in life. 'Don't do anything daft now,' had been her parting advice, intended to cover the proverbial multitude of sins. My Aunt Jessie had said I was a sensible lassie and given me a knowing wink. They had already forewarned me in the weeks preceding not to speak to strangers (how did they expect me to avoid it when I only knew two people in the whole of Canada, Phil and his friend Mike?), not to go out at night alone, not to take drink or drugs or go to nightclubs. They both had a vision of the whole of the North American continent as a sink of iniquity, culled largely from watching old Hollywood films. Canada was a healthy, wholesome country, I told my mother, less full of vice than Glasgow, but I could see she didn't believe me. Foreign parts were suspect in her mind.

Anyway, here I was, in foreign parts right enough, and alone, going through Customs and Immigration where the man seemed to think I was up to no good and questioned me persistently about my motives for coming, and then I trundled in the wake of the crowd to wait helplessly for my suitcases to appear down the chute on to the revolving platform below. It was like a rugby scrum for which I didn't feel strong enough so I waited until the crowd abated and I could get in closer. I was beginning to feel dizzy watching the circulating suitcases. A nice man lifted off my two cases and I headed for the way out, clutching – and dropping – my various pieces of hand luggage, to the entrance lounge where, presumably, Phil would be awaiting me.

I scanned the faces of the people who were crammed against the barrier anxiously searching for arriving friends and relatives. Every second someone got up on their toes, waved and shouted, 'Hi!' There seemed to be no sign at all of Phil. Then I heard a voice calling, 'Maggie!'

I turned with a smile and saw a stranger smiling at me whilst saying my name again. 'Hey, don't you recognise me? It's me, Mike.'

20

'Mike!' He'd shaved off his beard and his reddish fair hair was tidier than when I'd last seen him. I glanced over his shoulder. 'Where's Phil?'

'Oh, Phil. He couldn't make it, I'm afraid.'

Chapter 2

I spent my first hour in Toronto with Mike trying to get out of the car park. He'd parked his car, an ancient Chevy, as he described it, on the eighth floor so there were seven floors of cars trying to get out in front of us, and it was the rush hour. The cars all looked enormous to me. I sat for the first half-hour mesmerised, watching the long gleaming machines gliding by one after the other with their tail lights gleaming. After that I began to get restless and scratch my arms and legs, a sure sign of nervous irritation in me. It wasn't just the waiting to get out of this big concrete building, I knew that; there were all sorts of other doubts and questions buzzing around in my head like mad bees. But, apart from anything else, I *was* beginning to wonder if it was possible to spend the rest of the day there. We had to keep the engine running and the fumes were none too sweet. Mike muttered under his breath about the engine needing tuning and that he could be doing with a new clutch and gearbox. She was a great little car though, yes sir! He slapped the steering-wheel affectionately. The car was not all that little, whatever else it was.

After the first few minutes conversation faltered between us and all but died. He told me I'd see Phil later but didn't give an explanation for his absence at the airport. Gradually, we crept down, floor by floor, stalling from time to time, which made Mike curse. Naturally the car always stalled when he had a chance to move on. On the last floor we had a slight disagreement with another vehicle, a huge shining Cadillac which thought it had the right of way over an old battered heap like ours. Mike's Chevy got its nose bumped. He jumped out like a mad thing to examine the damage and everyone behind us stood on their horns.

'Bad?' I asked, as he came back in.

'Big dent.' He was gloomy, understandably. The Cadillac had already swept on out into the evening.

I said I was sorry, feeling that it was my fault, as if I'd brought bad luck to him. This trip of mine was beginning to look like a mistake from start to finish. Where *was* Phil? That was one of the questions that was hammering at my brain. 'Patience, lassie, patience,' Granny would have said, 'all in good time.' She had always seemed to have an infinite store of the stuff. A pity she hadn't passed some of that on to me! Some of her qualities I had inherited, like her stubbornness, but I had missed out on the patience, definitely.

At last we made it: we were outside in the fresh air. And it was raining. Boy, was it raining! The downpour was torrential, with drops of rain bouncing like hailstones from the roadway. The temperature didn't feel too high either. And here was I with my suitcases full of lightweight cotton clothes. I had even trailed round Glasgow buying cotton knickers in case it would be too hot to wear nylon.

'Gee Willakers!' said Mike. 'That's all we need. The windshield wipers don't work too well.'

They were certainly going to have a tough time coping with this amount of moisture. They laboured valiantly, creaking and faltering under the onslaught, but they couldn't manage to keep a patch of windscreen clear enough for Mike to see. After the first hundred or so terrifying yards in which I felt we were driving blind he had to pull into the side; we would just have to sit the downburst out.

'How was the flight then?' he asked me for the third time, having to shout slightly to be heard. And for the third time I told him all about the smoked salmon and the chicken and Liza Minnelli.

The rain continued to beat against the car windows and on the roof, concealing us from the rest of the world, a world that I had not yet clapped my eyes on. I certainly felt that bit about being a stranger in a strange land.

Mike sighed, and then attempted to be hearty. 'Some welcome to Toronto, eh? Never mind, it doesn't do this too often.'

That was good, I said. Again, silence. Not like me to be so silent, I could usually chatter on, but somehow I felt the whole inside of me stilled and quiet, as if I didn't know how to cope with the situation I'd found myself in. It was an unusual sort of situation for me, for apart from not understanding what the scene was with Phil, I was, I realised, almost totally at the mercy of what other people had decided for me. I would have to go where they saw fit, await their pleasure. I was not too good at awaiting other people's pleasure, preferring to make my own action. My fidgets increased. And then I gave myself a little talking to. It was early days – no, hours – yet, and I couldn't expect to call the shots all the time. 'You aye want your own way, Maggie McKinley!' How many times had I heard that in my life? Guilty, Your Honour! That was my usual plea.

Mike was looking at me. Had I been muttering aloud? Surely even if I had he couldn't have heard me over the sound of the rain. He cleared his throat; I saw, even though I didn't hear it. 'And what's new with you?' he asked.

24

'My granny died.'

'Gee, I'm sorry. You were kind of fond of your granny, weren't you?'

Yes, I was kind of fond of her. The rain continued to wash across the windscreen and window panes.

Mike said he remembered me speaking of her and then there had been a brooch, hadn't there? I had lost it up Strathcarron and Phil had found it. Yes, there had been a brooch, with a Cairngorm stone set in it, that had once belonged to my great-great-granny Margaret Ross. I still had it, in fact I was wearing it now, pinned to my shirt. Putting my hand over it, I felt comforted: it made me feel that I had brought a part of my granny with me.

The last time I saw her it was Hogmanay. I went up to stay in Inverness-shire for a week and we had a grand old time together. I baked black bun and shortbread and cleaned her house and on Hogmanay itself we had a party, with all the old folks in from round about. The Frasers had been at their cottage too, but I did not see James. The snow had been good, and whenever I looked out at the white hills I thought of him skiing down their soft slopes, his cheeks whipped pink by the wind, his blue eyes clear and bright.

His mother called one day with a present for Granny: a pot of flowers. She stopped for a cup of tea and had a piece of my black bun, which she declared to be excellent.

'And how are you then, Maggie?' She spoke brightly, as was her wont, and I felt sure that she was relieved that the whole business had been broken off between James and me. It was enough for her to have her daughter married without having the son do the same thing.

I asked after Catriona and Mrs Fraser said that she was very well, which told me nothing. We chatted for a while, both of us carefully avoiding the mention of James's name.

And then Granny said, 'And how's young Jamie? Doing fine at the university, I expect?'

'Oh, very well indeed, very well. He's been working hard. No distractions!' Mrs Fraser gave a little tinkly laugh, the laugh that I had disliked on many occasions before.

And yet, that Hogmanay, I still missed seeing the Frasers and going to their cottage. My estrangement from James kept me away, too, from the glen. I longed to take the path that led between the high fir trees, along the side of the loch, and watch the hills come closer and closer. Some mornings, when I drew back the curtains and looked over in that direction, I felt the desire like a physical ache inside me. That visit was unlike my other ones up there, in that I spent my time almost completely with Granny and her friends. I did Mr Farquharson's laundry and he came to lunch every day and I listened to Mrs Clark's tales of her golden youth.

I meant to go back at Easter, I promised Granny that I would, but I hadn't been able to make it. We didn't get any holidays at the bookbinders and when it was the Glasgow Spring Holiday it seemed a terrible trail to go right up to Inverness-shire and down for the week-end. I wrote to Granny to tell her that I would come for a few days in June before I set off for Canada. 'Canada, lassie!' she had said when I had told her in January that I planned to go there. She had never been as far as Glasgow herself.

It rained for a solid hour, so I spent my second hour in Toronto with Mike sitting in his car waiting for the rain to pass.

When it slackened sufficiently for us to see the road again he said that he thought we could try making a dash for it. The freeway gleamed with wetness and the cars flashed past spraying water up from under their wheels. I felt terrified by the speed and the number of cars and the width of the lanes. I slid right down in my seat until my nose was level with the dashboard.

Mike seemed to drive competently enough though I was no judge of good or bad drivers. But we arrived safely in the centre of Toronto.

The first thing that struck me were the skyscrapers. I should have expected them to be so high but somehow I thought they would be more or less like our high-rise blocks of flats at home, but they were much higher. Mike pointed out various buildings to me and told me their heights which I immediately forgot. I *was* impressed by the height and the speed and the size of everything, even though I had been mentally prepared. Of course this was a big continent and I came from a small country.

We found somewhere to park and set off on foot into the cool dark evening. I shivered a little. What had happened to that humid heat I'd been warned about?

'I expect you're hungry?'

I had to confess that I couldn't eat another bite, not before I had a good long walk and shaken some of the food in my stomach down a bit. He laughed at that and the tension eased a little between us. For there had been tension ever since we'd met; we were almost like strangers who had been thrown together against our wills. Had Phil made him come and meet me because he didn't want to come himself?

Mike suggested we go for a walk round the town, and then when I was hungry we could take in a steak. I said that sounded great. Yonge and Bloor are the two main streets in Toronto; they cross at one point and then go on for miles, so Mike informed me. He spoke a little stiffly, like a guide taking a tourist round the city. I trotted beside him, listening, nodding, not taking in half of what he said.

27

Where *was* Phil? The streets were full of people sauntering along, out for the evening, and many of the shops, particularly those selling records and clothes, were still open. I liked the bustle and noise, and as we walked amongst the crowds I could feel myself relaxing and beginning to get interested. Yes, Mr Scott would have been right: after a bit I start to get interested.

And then the sky opened up again, sending people scurrying for doorways, where they stood packed together watching the rain dance and bounce on the pavements. It certainly seems to rain a lot here, I murmured, and Mike said it was proving to be an unusually wet summer. Trust me to pick a wet one when I'd hoped to go home with a deep brown tan that would be the envy of the street!

After a bit we made a dash for it and Mike took me to a café where they did good steaks. My piece of meat looked enormous although he said that that was just standard. But my appetite had recovered and I was able to make a good job of coping with it.

'That was good. Thanks a lot, Mike.'

'You're welcome!' He smiled at me. 'You look real neat, Maggie.'

'Neat?' I looked down at my crumpled cheesecloth shirt and washed-out jeans in astonishment. It was the first time I'd ever been called that.

He laughed at my surprise. 'I don't mean neat the way you mean it. We say it here to mean nice, cute, something like that.'

I laughed too, to cover my embarrassment at receiving a compliment from Mike. I hadn't been prepared for it. I hadn't been prepared for anything so far.

Where on earth was Phil?

It was now getting on for ten o'clock Toronto time, three o'clock a.m. Greenwich Mean Time. Back home my family would be snoring. I yawned.

'Tired?'

A little, I conceded, not too much. I wondered where I was going to spend the night. My job as an *au pair* would not begin for another week but Phil had said in one letter, a few weeks back, that he'd find somewhere for me to stay the week before. I didn't like to ask if they had made any arrangements.

'How would you like to go up to Ottawa tomorrow?' Mike asked. 'I've got a free week before I start my job as a lifeguard.'

I didn't know what to say so I mumbled something to suggest that that would be very nice. Did he mean go to Ottawa with him? Presumably?

'My mother would be real pleased to have you. And I've got three sisters.'

'Great!' And then I ventured to ask, 'And what's Phil doing?'

'Oh, he's working this week. He's got a job as a lifeguard too.'

'Oh, I see.' Our letters had tailed off in the last few weeks; Phil had been busy with his exams and I kept putting off writing thinking that it wouldn't be long now until we met and could tell one another all our news.

'More coffee?'

I shook my head. Mike said he would like some more so he got some. We continued to sit there. It was as if we were waiting for something to happen. From time to time he glanced at his watch so I wondered if perhaps he had arranged for Phil to come and meet us. But, somehow, I didn't like to ask. I felt I had to wait until I was given the information.

'We've arranged for you to spend the night with a girl,' said Mike rather hesitantly. 'She's called Lois.'

'Oh, I see.'

'Think we could head on out there now.'

We went back to the car and on the drive out he said that I'd probably have to make do with the floor, he hoped I wouldn't mind but they hadn't been able to arrange anything better. I said that I wouldn't mind at all, I'd be able to sleep on a log if I had to.

He drew up outside an old rambling dilapidated house, a rooming house, with about fifty-five names tacked on postcards on the front door. I followed him up an uncarpeted wooden stair to a door on which the one word was printed in flamboyant purple letters: LOIS. I had a sudden feeling of apprehension and sensed that I was not going to like Lois. Mike knocked, we heard a voice say, 'Come in!' and so we went in. And there was Lois, reclining on the settee with Phil.

I felt a hot flush spreading up from my neck over my cheeks. What a silly blithering idiot I had been! Did I think that because Phil had met me for one week last summer and been attracted to me that he was going to spend the whole year in-between not seeing any other girl, not having any girlfriends? Lois was very obviously his girlfriend.

He jumped up to greet me, also, I thought, with a little embarrassment. He seized my hand, saying it was great to see me again, and how was Scotland, etc.? There was only one place I wanted to be at that moment, and he'd just said the name of it.

I didn't take to Lois one bit. Of course I had plenty of reason not to. She was tall and willowy, blonde and languid, everything that I'm not. She towered above me, saying, 'Hi!' And that was it as far as she was concerned. She returned to smoking her cigarette and drinking the glass of wine that she held poised against her hip. Phil offered me some wine but I shook my head saying that I couldn't possibly drink another drop of anything. I felt deadbeat right from the soles of my feet to the top of my head. After all it would now be four o'clock in the morning by our own time back in Glasgow.

Mike and I squatted on cushions on the floor and they began to drink wine and talk, mostly about people I'd never heard of, naturally, so I sat mute and immobile. I kept my eyes well away from Phil. If only I could have crawled into a nice soft bed and cut out the world for a bit! My own bed for preference, with Jean snoring at the other side of the room. But I would have to lie here on the floor all night beside Lois.

I kept feeling myself drifting away, my eyelids sinking, and then I'd jerk back into consciousness, blink and take a look at these people, these strangers with whom I'd found myself.

Mike said, 'Hey, Maggie, you look done in.'

I tried to deny it but a large, uncontrollable yawn washed over me. I could have let myself go with it into oblivion.

Phil jumped up saying they'd be off and let us get to bed. I stared at his knees. There was a patch on one of them, sewn in red thread, badly. It wavered in front of me, blue and red swimming together.

'Have a nice trip then, Maggie,' said Phil.

I sensed that he was looking down at me but I did not look up. I nodded and they departed.

Lois hauled a piece of moth-eaten foam out of a cupboard, laid it on the floor and gave me an old quilt.

'Thanks,' I said.

'You're welcome,' she said, though I wondered if I were.

I went to the bathroom and washed my face, after which I collapsed on to the floor under the quilt and dropped into a soft, enveloping darkness.

*   *   *

During my week in Inverness-shire at Hogmanay I did take one day off. I hitched a lift up to Easter Ross. I wanted to go back and take another look at Strathcarron, whence my great-great-granny had been evicted in the 1850s, and, also, I wanted to have a look at Phil's stones. (He was going to be a geologist.) When he had left the hostel at Carbisdale Castle he had a huge collection of beautiful stones which he had been unable to take back to Canada on the plane, so he had presented them to me. I had wanted to bring them back to Glasgow but, what with the load being so enormous, and James being so annoyed at my taking them at all, I had had to unpack most of them. Carefully, I had erected a little cairn with the stones at the side of the road, and promised myself I would go back sometime to see if they were still there.

I got a lift right to Ardgay on the Easter Ross-Sutherland border, and then walked the last few miles up to Carbisdale Castle. It was a dry day, not too cold for late December, and overcast, but the air smelt sweet and I felt full of vigour and excitement to be back again. As I walked I remembered the time I'd spent there. I remembered Phil.

In the road below the hostel I came upon the cairn at the side of the road. It was intact. Kneeling down beside it, I let my hands run over the stones. It seemed an omen that it was still standing. To begin with I had intended to bring the stones back this time to Glasgow but now I saw it was better that they should stay where they were, as a monument to the time we had spent in this area together.

Sentimental fool, McKinley! Omens indeed! I awoke, thinking of Phil and his stones. I awoke to see Lois sprawled on her bed-settee, her blonde hair streaming out over the pillow, her right arm flung above her head. I had expected too much from Phil Ross and only had

32

myself to blame. I had built too much up out of our meeting. It had been too brief an encounter to last. Perhaps if I hadn't been working at the bookbinders, perhaps if I hadn't been so bored during all those months, then I might have got him, and us, into perspective. But I knew that I had built him up during those long hours so that I had had something nice to think about, to dwell on, to savour, and anticipate.

I got up and went to the window. The houses across the road looked similar to this one, fairly old, at least according to Canadian standards, I imagined, and they all had large verandahs around them. I liked the idea of a verandah, sitting on it watching people pass. Few of our houses in Scotland have verandahs. Different climate of course, different customs.

The sun was shining this morning and I'd had a good sleep. I would go to Ottawa with Mike and make the best of it. And to hell with Phil Ross!

Lois stirred and yawned, opening her eyes. 'Get some sleep?' she asked.

'Yes, thank you,' I answered primly, although I am not noted for my primness.

She got up and gave me a cup of instant coffee and a piece of rather dry bread: she had some coffee and a cigarette.

'Going off today with Mike, then, are you?'

I said yes. She observed that I must be pretty keen to have come all this way to see him and I said too hotly that I had come because I wanted to work in a different country. Keep the heid, McKinley! Take it easy, let yourself adjust slowly.

Dinne fash yersel', lassie!

Okay, Gran!

I was pleased though to see Mike when he arrived. He was more relaxed than he had been the previous evening

33

and so we set off together for Ottawa in fairly good spirits. Of Phil there was no sign, and no mention. I couldn't help but feel a bit annoyed that after the letters we'd exchanged and the encouragement he'd given me to come, he might at least have written to tell me about Lois so that I would have been forewarned. Or perhaps he'd thought that I wouldn't be expecting anything of him anyway?

The drive to Ottawa took about five hours and after the first part we were in wide open country with high trees and lakes. The scenery changed very little and I could see that in Canada you could drive for miles and miles without it changing much at all, whereas back home, in Scotland, every few miles the landscape could alter quite dramatically, so that one moment you were in moorland, the next in a glen, and the next in the mountains. This was a wide, vast country; I was beginning to get the feel of it. The roads were fairly empty; there was a lot of space for people.

We stopped beside a lake called Silver Lake to have a hamburger, and afterwards walked for a few minutes around the edge of the water. The smell of the pines was strong and delicious.

We continued the rest of the way to Ottawa, and it was only as we were driving into the outskirts that I began to think of the next step ahead. Mike's family. That was one body of people I had not reckoned on having to cope with. What would they be like?

'There's my mother!' said Mike suddenly, jamming on the brakes.

I looked but couldn't see anyone that might be his mother. We had drawn up just ahead of a woman, a rather large woman in small purple shorts and an orange and purple striped T-shirt, who was trotting along the edge of the road.

34

A little awkwardly, Mike said, 'She's into jogging these days.'

Mike's mother jogged up to the car and stopped, panting slightly, her hands on her hips. She looked hale and hearty, that I had to admit, and my eyes blinked rapidly. Into jogging! There were certainly going to be many different patterns of behaviour for me to observe here compared with back home. I could not imagine my mother or Aunt Jessie jogging through the streets of Glasgow in a pair of shorts.

Mike's mother said, 'So this is Maggie, eh? Your little Scottish girl?'

I blinked rapidly again. His little Scottish girl indeed! Did his family think that I had come as *his* girlfriend? She said they were delighted to welcome me here and she beamed upon me with great good nature. At least this was going to be a change from Mrs Fraser's sharp-eyed appraisal.

'Well, must get on and do my stint. See you later, Maggie!' And she was off, legs moving smoothly and steadily. I gazed after her, full of wonder and admiration.

'She's into a real health kick just now. A lot of people arc. What about in Glasgow?'

'Don't think it's reached there yet.'

Mike lived in a very nice house in a leafy street. Again, it was not new, and there had I been imagining, before I came, that everyone would live in brand-new shining houses over here. It was a wood-framed building with a lovely verandah and hanging pots of flowers. Seated on the verandah were Mike's three sisters, all sandy-haired and freckle-faced like himself. I could see at a glance that they were considerably younger than I.

I was introduced and the youngest giggled. She was frowned upon heavily by Mike and I felt sympathy for him, knowing what it was like to have younger siblings.

35

For a moment I felt the terrible pang of homesickness and wished that Jean and I could be sniping away at one another.

But Mike's family was nice, including his father who was another sandy-haired, freckled-nosed man. Indeed, they all seemed good-natured and open-hearted, fantastically so, and I was received immediately into the bosom of the family. His mother, Mrs Kennedy, started fairly soon to quiz me about vitamins and was horrified when she heard that I didn't take any at all. She said that I looked as if I could do with pepping up, particularly with iron. She reached over and pulled down my eyelid to see if I was bloodless. No doubt I was. I felt it.

'Do you drink plenty of milk?'

I confessed that I didn't like milk at all, which horrified her all the more. She said that I would have to get to like it, there was more goodness in a pint of milk than in any other food. They drank skimmed milk, so that there was no chance of imbibing too much cholesterol. Every single thing that was put on the table was examined for cholesterol potential, or ingredients that could cause all sorts of diseases. No vinegar since that was bad for the blood, nothing smoked, no blue cheese, etc. The list was endless, and the things that could happen to you if you took any of these things was so impressive that I wondered that my right ear hadn't dropped off already. Mrs Kennedy asked if my mother was conscious of food values and so forth. 'Not too much,' I said, thinking of my mother tucking into a good Scotch mutton pie with tinned beans. That would have been enough to make Mrs Kennedy drop dead in her tracks. Throughout the meal she delivered a lecture on what was good and what was bad to put into your stomach. Then she subjected me to a rigorous detailed cross-examination as to how much exercise I took and of what nature it was. I told her that I walked a lot.

'In the country?'

'Sometimes.' Most of the time it was through the streets of Glasgow, and I had the feeling that Mrs Kennedy would not approve of that. But in spite of this crazy obsession (okay, crazy to me, maybe not to them!) she was nice and I didn't really mind; I just sat and nodded as if I agreed and opened my mouth when she wanted to pop a vitamin pill inside. She strongly recommended that I take up jogging; it appeared to be the remedy for many ills. Everyone was into jogging these days, she told me, and she felt now that she couldn't live without it.

I was given a bedroom to myself, for which I was profoundly grateful. I went to bed early and wrote a long letter to my family. 'Dear all,' I wrote, 'here I am in Canada, the land of the maple leaf and the Mountie! I haven't clapped eyes yet on a Mountie and I don't know if I've seen a maple leaf.' I'm so dead useless when it comes to identifying trees that someone has to take me right up to one, point and say, 'There!' Although the maple leaf has a very distinctive shape, I had to admit that. I sat gazing out at the verandah of the house across the way, at the old couple rocking themselves to and fro in the evening sunshine, and wondered what else I could write. I couldn't tell them about Lois, or Phil, and they hadn't even heard of Mike so I couldn't write that I was now spending a week with Mike's family in Ottawa. The safest thing was a description of the place and all the food we had eaten. Smoked salmon and asparagus! Maggie's fairly living it up, that's what they would say, and I only wished that I could be there to hear them say it. Oh, shut up, McKinley, quit havering and giving way to such soppy homesickness. Enjoy yourself! That's what you're here for!

When I slept I dreamt and in my dream I was in Easter

Ross. My granny was sitting at the side of the road and I was picking up the stones from the cairn, the one that I had built, and throwing them in all directions. She was trying to say something to me but I could not quite make out what it was that she said.

I awoke thinking that she was still alive, and was again faced with the realisation that she was not. That was one of the hardest things I was finding out: the awakening every morning to face the fact anew that my granny was dead.

'Have you got a pain or something?'

I jerked up my head to see the child in the doorway. 'Who are you?' I demanded, bewildered.

'Christine. Mike's sister.'

Of course, who else? Mike's sister. The trouble was that I had travelled so far and so quickly that I couldn't quite keep abreast with what was happening to me.

'Better get up,' she said. 'Mom's mixing up the yoghurt and muesli.'

'Tea and toast's all I eat in the morning,' I bleated.

'You don't think you'll get away with that, do you?' she said cheerfully. Then she gave me a quick, toothless grin and somersaulted out of the room.

Chapter 3

Fortified with honey, yoghurt and muesli, and my digestive system unsullied by such nasty killer foods as white bread or white sugar, I set out daily with Mike to see the sights of Ottawa and district. It was a beautiful city with its Parliament buildings, canal, two rivers, the Ottawa and the Rideau, tree-lined avenues, handsome mellow-looking brick houses with nice verandahs and trim unfenced lawns in front. Even the big houses in posh districts had no fences. In Scotland we tend to like stone walls round our properties. A different custom reflecting a different way of looking at yourself and your neighbour presumably. Mike grinned at my 'social anthropological' comments, as he called them.

We were getting on much more easily together now. Phil was seldom mentioned between us although I still thought of him. Oh yes, I certainly did, and when I did I felt a dull ache deep inside me. Most of the time I tried not to think about him. I tried to concentrate on the present and present company.

It was amazing how clean everything was. The lack of litter constantly surprised me. 'I guess Glasgow's pretty dirty, eh?' said Mrs Kennedy. She knew all about the crime rate, heart attack incidence, delinquency, and so on. Mike said she read a lot of magazines which gave out potted information. But she was okay and nice and kind to me though I couldn't help wondering what Phil's mother would have been like. It was her I had expected to meet if I'd met anybody's mother. Forget him, McKinley! He's forsaken you for Lois of the long legs and long golden hair and who can blame him? We had made no promises to one another.

Mike's father worked for the Government. More than half the people in Ottawa were civil servants. For his health kick he did weightlifting in the basement.

The girls were not bad as girls of their age went, although Christine, the youngest, I could have managed without. She kept cartwheeling a couple of inches from my nose and when she came to rest she would ask me with an air of put-on dumbness if I was crazy about Mike? She also told me that she thought my skin looked kind of yellow, like a Chinese. All the natives in Glasgow had yellow skins, I told her, and ate haggis every day along with several slices of pre-packaged white bread liberally sprinkled with white sugar. She told her mother who appeared to believe it, the bit about the haggis and the white bread anyway, for she told me she wasn't one bit surprised, it explained a lot.

So, with a bit of misunderstanding and crossed lines and quite a bit of communication also, my first week in Canada was passed in the bosom of Mike's family. Another week there and I'd have probably been into jogging and buttermilk.

Most days we got around quite a bit in Mike's old Chevy. 'Anywhere in particular you'd like to go?' Mike asked casually the first morning, not knowing what he was letting himself in for. 'Just a minute,' I told him, I had to fetch my notebook. He stared at it in amazement, at the page after page of scrawled notes. I'd been reading up about the Scots in Canada, wanting to know the other side of the story – I already knew about the Scots as emigrants and the reasons for their going.

Mike stared at me now. 'I knew the Scots had left their mark on Canada, but listening to you, Maggie, I'm beginning to understand why!'

We went exploring, with me holding the map and Mike chauffering, as he put it. 'Anything you say, mam. Where to next?' At times I saw that look on his face that had been there when Phil Ross and I went in pursuit of our ancestors last summer in Easter Ross and then I'd give over a bit and say let's do what you want to do, which was usually swimming in one of the lovely lakes in the Gatineau Hills, and that was fine with me too, except if it was late afternoon and the mosquitoes were out. They were absolute monsters and had a good few meals off me although I didn't know why since I'm not over-endowed with meat on my bones. 'It's your blood they're after,' said Mike with relish. Vampire insects! I had thought the midges in the Scottish Highlands were bad enough until I encountered those beasts. I came up in huge, hard-centred yellow lumps that nearly drove me crazy. Mosquitoes became my number one enemies and I was constantly on the look-out for them. In the evenings, when the family congregated on the verandah, I sat inside, safely tucked away behind screened doors and windows and watched them getting bitten. Okay, coward! I pleaded guilty. As I see it, there's no point in suffering if you don't have to.

One day, when I was buying postcards in a small town in Dundas County, the woman behind the counter said to me, 'You Scotch?' 'Yes! How did you know?' She smiled. Her great-grandmother had come from Scotland. Well, fancy that! Mike groaned and drifted out on to the sidewalk. I let him go and had a nice wee chat. As far as I was concerned, chats were part of travelling. The woman told me that her great-grandmother had been evicted

41

from Strathnaver during the Highland Clearances. I was immediately interested, of course.

'Dreadful, wasn't it?' I said.

'Ah well, maybe it was at the time but perhaps in the end it was all for the best.' It was, in her great-granny's case, it seemed. They had had a hard time trying to make a living from the land, the soil was so thin; yet if they hadn't had to go they might never have budged. 'She came to Canada with her husband and they did very well for themselves.'

So this was a new aspect of the Clearances for me to think on. That is the marvellous thing about history: every event has so many facets. There is seldom any absolute truth.

'Well,' said Mike, when I rejoined him, 'have you finished talking about your grannies yet?'

I dunked him in the ribs.

He said that he had just the place lined up for me for our last day, though he didn't know if he was wise taking me to it.

It was a museum community called Upper Canada Village which had been set up to recreate the life, work and development of the early settlements in the upper St Lawrence valley. The building of the Seaway meant that eight villages had to be flooded. They saved some typical houses and other buildings such as schools, churches and barns, with their furnishings and equipment, and brought them to this one place on the river to form the core of a museum village.

It looked just like a real mid-nineteenth-century village, and the roads, gardens and fences, livestock, poultry and out-buildings were all historically accurate. And it was peopled with men and women dressed in the costumes of the time performing the tasks that they would have then, such as making cheese or butter or bread,

42

weaving or spinning, or sewing quilts.

I liked the village a lot, felt it was not artificial even though I knew it had been artificially contrived and brought together, but it had a feeling of reality about it; history, in fact, had been brought to life. The roads were gravelled, as they would have been then, and whenever it rained they were inclined to turn muddy; there were weeds in the back lanes and no one had tried to manicure the place or turn it into a stage set; and there were vegetable patches outside the back doors of the houses with vegetables growing in them. 'Yes,' said Mike, 'real vegetables.' He smiled at my enthusiasm and reached out to tuck a piece of hair back from my face. My hair has a habit of escaping in all directions. I looked away from his eyes.

It rained quite a bit during our visit, off and on, which, somehow, made it seem more realistic for, as we scuttled through the back lanes in the rain getting our feet wet in the long grass and took shelter in a barn, it made me feel that we might have been two inhabitants of the village long ago. Standing inside looking out, with the old farm implements behind us, I could well imagine we *were* inhabitants, on our way to Crysler's Store to have our flour and sugar weighed out, to purchase a piece of calico and some patent medicines, to natter about village gossip over the scored wooden counter. Who had come in on the stagecoach? Who was staying at Cook's Tavern or Willard's Hotel? I had a longing, almost like a pang of homesickness, for a way of life, a community life, of a kind that I had never experienced. Funny that it should come to me like a wave of homesickness since I had never experienced it, but perhaps, who knows, it had come to me out of my ancestral memory? In our old area of Glasgow we had known everyone but not in the way that people would have done in a village like this. There must have been a tight cosy feeling generated within the confines of a settlers' village, all pulling together, interdependent, each one with a well-defined and vital role. Cheesemaker, baker, blacksmith, doctor, teacher, farmer, cabinetmaker, candlemaker, broom-maker, pastor. All strong roles central to life. I bet no one then thought about studying social anthropology!

The rain slackened. Mike took my hand and we walked on to the doctor's house.

'It must have been a peaceful, satisfying life,' I said.

Mike shrugged. 'Maybe. But limiting too.'

I could have spent hours in each house, soaking up the atmosphere, imagining life going on. Mike had to drag me from one building to the next. He said that at this rate we'd be here till the next morning. I wouldn't have minded. I would have loved to have checked in at Cook's Tavern and slept in one of the guest rooms and got up in the morning to wash my face in cold water in the china basin. The beds looked hard, Mike said, but I told him that that wouldn't have bothered me. He said he didn't think I'd have been a sentimentalist. I was not, I protested: my desire was not in the least sentimental. I felt quite irritated by him, although he remained, as always, good-humoured, and didn't seem to register my irritation. He was, in fact, teasing me in his own fashion. But his remarks about hard beds and no electricity and no sidewalks were the kind of prosaic, down-to-earth remarks that I suspected Phil would not have made. Suddenly I realised that they were the very kind of remarks that James Fraser would have made.

That day after the funeral James and I walked, hand in hand, right up to the head of the glen in Inverness-shire, as we had done many times in the past. We passed the farm, the cows drinking down at the bend of the burn under the hump-backed bridge, the old abandoned burnt-out cottages, including the wreck of my great-great-granny Margaret Ross's; we passed all these familiar things but I looked at each one with new eyes as if I had never seen them properly before. The whole world seemed sharper, as if it were outlined in black and a strong light beaming down on it. Strange. I commented on this to James and he said that maybe death made you more conscious of life.

The peace filled me and when we reached the head of the glen and sat down together I was glad that I had left the rest of the family and come back up here. We gazed back down to where the old schoolhouse, now the Frasers' holiday house, and the burnt-out shell of my granny's old cottage stood close together on opposite sides of the narrow grey road. There was a lot of history attached to this glen. There was a lot of history here even for James and me.

We were in tune. I felt that he knew what I was thinking without having to say it or ask. We had always been greatly in tune together. I sighed.

'Try not to fret too much, Maggie,' he said, not realising I was thinking more of him than my granny. 'She wouldn't have wanted you to be sad, I'm sure.'

Why shouldn't I be sad? Why shouldn't I grieve? I had lost my grandmother and that was a big event in my life. She herself would have understood that.

James squeezed my hand and then slid his arm around me and held me tight against his shoulder. 'I'm so glad I've found you again, Maggie,' he said.

'Hey!' said Mike, shaking my hand, which he still held. 'You looked as if you'd gone miles away. Were you back in the past?'

'Guess I was.' I laughed.

45

It was easy to slip back and at times I felt the past and present closely intermingled.

The air smelt sweet and fresh after the rain and I took a deep breath filling my lungs. 'I wish I could get a chance to work on something like this, to recreate a way of life out of the past.'

'What on earth made you want to take up social anthropology?'

I started to explain, or try to. Wasn't it always difficult to say exactly why one decided to do anything, what one's motives were? Mike said he didn't think so: he had decided to do physics because he liked physics. It was as simple as that, but for me it couldn't have been that simple because I didn't know if I would like social anthropology or not. Well, I told him, to be honest, initially, the name had intrigued me and it was something different, something that no one else in my school was considering doing.

'Aha! I thought as much. That's a very flimsy reason to base your life on, Maggie McKinley.'

But that wasn't all, that wasn't the end of it, not by any means. I went on to enthuse about the famous anthropologist Margaret Mead who had gone alone to Samoa to study adolescence in the days when the boats only called there once every three weeks or something like that, certainly long before they had a jet landing strip. As they did now, of course, to bring in the American tourists. 'And then she went to New Guinea when they were still hunting heads—'

'That's all very well. *Was* all very well. For her. But the world's different now.'

I was silent, for a second, as I watched the old stagecoach pass by on its journey through the village. It was laden up with tourists.

'Yes, okay.' I knew what he meant: there *were* landing

strips for jets now in most places, most primitive peoples had been subjected to so-called civilisation, but there were still places to go, people to study, cultures to compare. Not everything was known. Never would be, I hoped!

'But what'll you do after you have your degree?'

I didn't know and didn't care that I didn't know. I was content to wait for each part of my life to evolve and felt sure that, as it did, one thing would lead out of another. I felt that I could see my life spreading outwards a bit like a fan, but it wasn't mapped out, as James Fraser's more or less was. That had been one of the reasons that I had broken with him in the first instance. Phil would be more like me, I fancied. The thought brought that ache again, the tug inside. If he had been here I wouldn't have had to explain.

'Come on now, no need to look so gloomy about it. I didn't mean to attack you or anything. I'm sure you'll make out just fine with it.'

Outside the white wooden church horses were cropping the grass contentedly. We went inside, found a feeling of order and balance. It was a clean bright place. The pews were fenced off like pens and I presumed that each family would have had its own one.

Mike and I sat down for a while.

'Remember the church at Croick?' He laughed.

Did I remember it? How could I not? Phil, Mike and I had spent a night lying on its floor, whilst James had been floundering around lost on the hills in mist. This church with its bright white cleanness was a different matter from that dour old Scottish Presbyterian one, set in a hollow and surrounded by yew trees and old gravestones. I said I thought I would prefer to spend a night here, if I had to spend another night in a church.

'How is James anyway?'

I shrugged, said he was okay.

And then Mike said, 'I guess you and he are not—? Well, not going steady any more?'

'No,' I said, 'we're not.'

My family spent the night after Granny's funeral in her flat. The next day we were going to pack up her things, throw some stuff out and keep one or two bits and pieces. Most of what she had was of no value, being second-hand and purchased by Mrs Fraser and me at auctions, as most of Granny's possessions had been lost when her house went up in flames.

I slept on the settee, whilst my mother and father slept in Granny's bed in the bedroom. All night I tossed and turned, waking, drenched with perspiration from time to time, thinking about my granny and about James, and the two seemed to be intertwined.

What had I done to James? I had done something terrible, I knew that, even in the middle of my uneasy slumber. I had led him to believe I would become his steady girlfriend again, I had given him hope. And I knew that I had done it because of my granny's death, because I had needed someone to turn to, and he had happened to be there and was a suitable person.

In the morning I got up early, more exhausted than when I had lain down. I went out just as the cocks were starting to crow. The air was cool and nipped at my face. I was appalled now at what I had done, or rather at what I had let happen. It had seemed to have gone out of my control at some point. I had been too weak, too low in spirit to prevent it. And now? Now I had to face the fact that I must tell James Fraser for the second time that I did not want to pledge myself to him for ever, that I wanted to be, must be, free.

*   *   *

'I really liked Scotland,' Mike was saying. 'Especially the North. I'd sure like to get back sometime.'

'Phil always said—' I decided to be brave, now that I had pronounced his name, and make myself continue '—Phil always said he'd like to come back to Scotland too, that it was a geologist's paradise.'

'Guess he might, sometime.' Mike did not appear to want to discuss that topic.

We moved on to the Ross-Boffin House (built by Thomas Ross – those Rosses were everywhere!). Inside, two women were demonstrating the making of a quilt. The process fascinated me. I watched the women ply their needles in and out, creating a fantastically beautiful pattern of lilies, working on each square separately and then fitting it on to a wooden frame. I questioned them and listened carefully, nodding my head, and all the time I was thinking that when I went back to Scotland I would make one myself. Yes, I would! I knew full well what my mother would say. 'You, Maggie McKinley, sit and sew! That'll be the day.' But it would be the day, I was determined about that, I would make a quilt and it would be my Canadian Settler Quilt, a relic of a past culture, and I would put it on my bed in my Edinburgh bed-sit when I went up to university. Eventually, seeing how bored Mike was looking, I had to go.

'You're fifty times worse than my sisters,' he said, smiling. 'I thought it was bad enough the last time I brought them here, but you!'

In the craft shop I bought a pair of moccasins and an exquisite Eskimo stone carving of a seal. They were going to be the beginnings of my collection which I would bring back from different countries, from different cultures. I also bought several bars of soap which were made in the village, a loaf of the home-baked bread, which weighed a ton, and a lump of the cheese.

'Anything else you'd like to take back with you?'

'Heaps of things, but I can't afford them.' I would come back another day, another time, another year.

We were the last to leave the village when they closed up for the night. As we walked back to the car park together I turned to Mike and said, 'It's been a fantastic day. I've really enjoyed myself. And I hope you haven't been too bored, Mike?'

'Bored? I don't feel bored when I'm with you, Maggie.'

How nice he was! Impulsively, I reached up and kissed him, in what I hoped was an affectionate, sisterly sort of way. But as soon as I drew back I sensed from the look on his face that I had made a mistake. Quickly I began to gabble about quilt-making, and how I intended to begin as soon as I got to Toronto.

On our way back to Ottawa we stopped at a roadside joint for a hambuger, then drove on into the city. Mike said I hadn't seen the Parliament buildings yet, how about doing that tonight? He seemed in no mood to go home and rejoin the bosom of his family.

We made the last tour of the Parliament for that evening. Obediently, we trotted around in the wake of the guide listening to the details of its history. It was a very fine building and I enjoyed seeing it.

'You're good to take places,' said Mike. 'You enjoy yourself so much.'

As we came out the lights were coming on in the valley below and in the tall buildings round about. The air had a kind of magical sparkle about it which made me want to skip. I love night-time in a city. We took the path that wound its way around the edge of the cliff top. There was a sound of music: a group was giving a concert down by the river bank. In front of us black streams rose up into the air.

'What are those?' Instinctively, I drew back.

'Mossies.' Mike laughed.

I shivered and he slid his arm around my waist, pulling me towards him. He told me softly not to worry about mosquitoes, they might nibble me a bit but they weren't likely to do me much harm, not in the long run. Then he nibbled my right ear. I pretended not to notice. That seemed the best way to cope with the situation, or rather my instinct told me to ignore it since that was usually my first impulse when anything was unwelcome. I defintely didn't want to have my ear nibbled by Mike, much as I liked him. And I did like him a lot but, to use an overworked phrase, simply as a good friend. I couldn't see what was wrong in having a good friend once in a while even if he happened to be male rather than female, and I'd hoped that Mike was going to fall into that category. I'd found it a difficult category to establish when it came to making male friends. I even wondered, as we sauntered on, lopsided now, with me anxiously scanning the valley and talking gaily of the music, and Mike half-leaning over my head trying to gaze into my dark-veiled eyes, if he thought he ought to make romantic overtures to me, if he thought that I would consider him abnormal if he didn't.

'It's a real nice night,' he murmured, breathing against the right side of my neck. It felt like a blast off the Kalahari.

'Neat.' I laughed, nervously. Please, Mike, don't bother, I wanted to say to him, but how could I?

Suddenly, he grabbed me, almost knocking me off balance, and kissed me, in a manner that could either be described as fiercely or clumsily, depending on the way you wanted to look at it. There was no question about my point of view.

'Gee, Maggie! It's great you came to Canada.'

'Look, Mike,' I began.

'Uh-huh?'

'You didn't have to, you know.'

'Have to what?'

'Well, kiss me.'

'But I wanted to, you dumb nut!' His voice was warm and teasing. 'I know I didn't *have* to.'

'Oh, I see.'

My voice was obviously not warm at all, or teasing, for he let his arm slacken slightly around my waist, and his voice changed, taking on a slight edge. 'Didn't you want me to? Is that what you're trying to say?'

The mosquitoes came to save me: at that moment I was bitten very sharply on the ankle, and then on the nape of the neck, and then the cheek. Retribution no doubt. One of those nasty black swarms was upon us. I didn't wait to explain, I fled, without any further warning. He followed, demanding to know what in the name I thought I was playing at. Presumably he had not even noticed the mosquitoes. I gasped out a few words about being bitten to death, whilst I batted my hands around my head and kept moving. But he wasn't having any, he wasn't going to accept such a simple explanation. As he pursued me he kept repeating that I hadn't wanted him to kiss me, had I? Had I? 'Shush, Mike,' I said, but he wouldn't shush, he was as mad as hell, as mad as those swarming insects in pursuit of my blood.

We were out on the pavement now, and seemed to have left the swarm behind us. I stopped for breath. I had a stitch in my side, apart from about ten thousand bites all over my body. He repeated his question. I hadn't wanted him to kiss me, had I? Surely that was a plain enough question and I could give a plain enough answer, damn me! It was funny, that before, when I had met Mike in Scotland, I never thought he would have been this intense: he had always played things very casually, as if he saw life as a great joke from beginning to end. Now here he was standing in front of me demanding an answer to his silly question. I did think it was a silly question, the kind that you didn't ask anyone.

'Now, listen, Mike—'

'I'm listening.' He sounded grim.

So okay, maybe I hadn't wanted him to kiss me, but did that have to be a part of any relationship between a male and a female? I tried to explan to him how I felt about platonic relationships, and how I felt about him and valued his friendship. We stood there on the sidewalk with people swerving around giving us a wide berth for we obviously looked as if we were in the middle of a row. It was ridiculous and I wanted to stamp my foot. I didn't want this degree of involvement. The night was cooling now and I wished I'd brought a cardigan. He stood before me, legs apart, looking as stolid as a Mountie on guard, not moving, not prepared to move, not even twitching an eyebrow, as far as I could tell. I began to think longingly of the peace in a village such as the one we had seen this afternoon and how relaxing it would be to sit and make a quilt with a bunch of other women.

'Look, Mike, let's be friends.'

'It's Phil, isn't it?'

It was easier to say yes than no; I wasn't even sure whether it had anything to do with Phil or not; maybe it did, and maybe it didn't. But even if Phil hadn't existed and even if I hadn't kind of liked him, which I had to admit to myself that I did, I didn't think I'd have wanted to get involved with Mike in the way that he so obviously wanted. I sighed and said, 'I guess so.' At least that would probably settle the matter.

Now he sighed. 'Nothing more for me to say then.'

We said nothing more on the way home, and in the morning left Ottawa after his mother had drawn me aside to tell me that she was real pleased to have met Mike's girl, she'd always suspected he'd had a girl tucked away somewhere – surely not Scotland? – and they had all liked me a lot, etc. I had liked them a lot too, I told her in return, without being able to let her know that I didn't like her son enough, or not in the right way for him, or her. What a mixed-up scene! Why couldn't Phil have met me fancy-free at the airport as I had anticipated, as I had imagined? I had lived out the scene many times during the winter months: our reunion at Toronto airport. Well, it hadn't worked out that way, and he hadn't been fancy-free when I arrived in Toronto, and so that was that.

'Remember to keep taking your honey,' said Mrs Kennedy, and I promised that I would, and thus we parted, she getting ready to go off on a jog, whilst I looked like a measles patient, covered with angry-looking lumps well daubed with calamine lotion. They had even attacked my face last night and I was such a ghastly-looking sight that I could hardly believe Mike would still fancy me. But I didn't look at his face to find out whether he did or not.

The five hours back to Toronto seemed more like fifty. From time to time I made an attempt at casual conversation, praising the glories of the Canadian countryside, but Mike would not be drawn. He was every bit as moody as James Fraser was capable of being.

'I don't believe you care for anyone but yourself,' James told me. 'You're scared to let yourself feel anything.'

'That's not true! I feel all sorts of things—'

'This is the second time—'

'I know, I know! Don't rub it in, please.'

'Don't rub it in, she says! How do you think I feel?'

'I've tried to explain, that what with my granny's death—'

'For heaven's sake, Maggie, grow up. You can't be tied

54

to your granny all your life.' And then he apologised stiffly, saying that he shouldn't have said that and he had not meant to offend me, but didn't I think my tie with her had been a bit unnatural?

No, I told him, equally stiffly, most certainly not. And I went on to say that I thought there was something wrong with him that he should think so; other kinds of love existed in the world besides romantic or sexual love. Now we both sounded like pompous asses, and so we had our last meeting, standing under a sweet-smelling Douglas fir tree on a fine June morning, glaring at one another with hatred.

'Mike,' I said with desperation as we approached the outskirts of Toronto, 'don't you think friendship's important? Good solid friendship without any kind of sex having to come into it? That kind often lasts longer than the other, you know.'

He shrugged as if he didn't care, or know; but he did not give me any answer which made me feel immensely sad. James Fraser had told me, just before we parted, that he hoped he would never have to set eyes on me again for the rest of his life.

Chapter 4

We met Phil in Toronto. Obviously an arrangement had been made that we should meet but I was not told until we actually came upon him. We met up with him on the corner of Yonge and Bloor.

'Hi! Had a good week?'

'Great,' I said.

Mike said nothing.

'Well, shall we go eat?' said Phil. We went and ate in a hamburger joint. By the time I left Canada I would look like a cross between a hot dog and a hamburger. I had never eaten so many of either in my life before but had to admit that they were a lot better than the ones back home. We spread our hamburgers with mustard and relish and piled them up with salad and munched. They were so thick we could concentrate on the eating and didn't have to do too much talking, which was just as well since none of us seemed to have much to say.

When we finished Phil said he wanted to hear about everything we'd done, so I, in a false bright voice, related a list of the week's events.

'I'm glad you had such a good time. Wish I could have been there with you.'

Did he mean that? Or was he just being polite? He hadn't mentioned Lois since we'd met him but that, of course, meant nothing. He said he'd had a pretty good week himself, the sun had shone most of the time and nobody had tried to drown themselves. His skin was tanned a deep brown and I couldn't help thinking how handsome he looked. Control yourself, McKinley, and just don't let yourself look at him! But I didn't want to look at Mike either! There was nothing else for it but to stare down at the table which didn't do much for my morale. Grease-stained formica.

It turned out that the boys were going to take me to my place of work that evening. Phil presumed that I knew all about it, so I sat and kept silent. During the course of the evening Mike said not more than two or three sentences and after a bit Phil began to notice and glance at him uneasily. Then I saw him take a glance back at me. He was wondering if we'd quarrelled. Well, let him wonder! In the end we were all sitting uneasily half-silent over our dirty plates and cups. What had happened to the rapport that had existed amongst us in northern Scotland last summer? Okay, okay, I know you can't relive old times: that seemed to be the obvious message. Things seldom work out the same the second time round, I ought to have known that, but I am eternally hopeful.

My new employers, who were called Willoughby, lived in a large expensive house in a quiet, leafy suburb of Toronto. The boys drove me out there. The door was opened by a middle-aged woman with a thick European accent. She turned out to be Czech and the house-keeper. Her name I never did master and I could certainly not begin to spell it. She fetched Mrs Willoughby and withdrew.

Mrs Willoughby smiled with her mouth; her eyes were too busy working me over, assessing me. She was glossy, as if covered with a thin coat of varnish that would chip if you scratched it with your fingernail, and her hair stood out stiff and proud about her head. You could almost see the drops of lacquer on each strand. Later, I learned that she owned and ran an expensive boutique downtown (her husband was in some other business). Mr Scott was always saying that I was bad at making snap judgements, I should wait and I'd often find a person or an idea was not quite as I thought at first meeting. This was another instance in which I didn't wait.

'Give us a call if you need anything then, Maggie,' said Phil, backing away down the drive. 'You've got our number?'

I couldn't imagine myself giving them a call for anything, knowing that Phil had Lois around and Mike wouldn't want to hear from me, even if I was in the last throes of desperation.

'I'll just show you your room then, dear,' said Mrs Willoughby, and proceeded up the thick pile carpeted stairs in front of me. The room was nice enough, I had to admit that, and there was even a small portable T.V. on the bedside table. The children were all in bed, she explained. She had expected me earlier in the day.

'Never mind, at least you're here now. You're fond of kids, eh?'

Oh yes, yes indeed. I could hardly have said anything else since I was there to like them, but the truth was I had never been too keen. Perhaps hers would change my mind. She told me about them: Roland was ten, exceedingly intelligent and very, very observant (that was a bit of an understatement, as I was to find out), Tracey was six and real cute, and Elmer was just three, and an absolute pie. She was sure that they would be no trouble at all to me, no one had ever found them to be naughty or bothersome, not for a second. She actually had the nerve to look me in the eye as she said these things. Then she gave me a little pep talk about things like cleanliness and attention to duty and said that she was prepared to treat me well if I gave her her money's worth in return. Fair enough. That was something I could agree to.

Then she went off, leaving me alone in my new room. If I was hungry I should go down and raid the icebox; I was to make myself at home.

Phil had brought me my mail which I now took out and read. There was a big bulky letter from my family, which was not at all like them. They're famous for their five-line epistles. 'We are all well, hope you are too. . . .' I ripped it open. Inside was a second envelope, edged with red, white and blue. Pulling it out, I saw the Canadian stamp, and my name, 'Miss Maggie McKinley', and turning it over the name and address of sender: 'Mr Phil Ross'. I looked at the postmark and calculated backwards. It had been sent a week before I left Glasgow.

My fingers fumbled opening this envelope. I drew out a thin sheet of paper.

'Dear Maggie,' he had written. 'This is a letter I should have written before but I guess I've been putting off. It's kind of difficult to write and I don't know exactly how to put it. The fact is I have a girl, her name's Lois, and we've been going pretty steady since Easter. I just thought I should let you know.

'I hope this won't make any difference to you coming to Canada. I'm sure you'd enjoy the trip. . . .'

I stared out at the heavy dark green trees that concealed the house from the road. Would it have made any difference if I had got the letter before I left? I wasn't sure. It might, and then again I might have been more determined to come and enjoy Canada and think to hell with Phil Ross! But if I had got it then at least I'd have been prepared. There were only another two or three stilted lines before he signed his name. It must have been an awkward letter to write and I imagined he'd written it more than once. It didn't read as if it had been written spontaneously.

So he'd thought when we met that I knew. I tried to think back, with hindsight, over our two meetings, but the overwhelming mood that had coloured them had been one of awkwardness. We had certainly not 'clicked' this time. I sighed.

Now I unfolded the family's letter. It had been written half by my mother and half by Jean, with a long P.S. from Aunt Jessie. My mother began by saying that the letter from Canada had come in the post just after I'd left for Prestwick. Then she went on to tell me how everyone was getting on and how the business was doing. Everything was normal: the family had their usual troubles and the business was rocking on its feet, on the brink of bankruptcy. My dad was so fidgety in the evenings that she ended up taking a tranquilliser herself as often as not. When I was at home I did my best to hide the bottle from her. It was all right for some, she finished up, meaning me of course. If she could have seen me sitting there in that strange pale-pink silken room in Toronto, surrounded by strangers, with a suggestion of moisture around my eyes, she mightn't have been so ready to say it. Ah well, they'd all still be there when I got back, and when I did I'd probably find them a pain in the neck with their griping and moaning.

I had another letter, from Catriona, the sister of James Fraser.

'You'll never guess, Maggie,' wrote Catriona, 'I'm expecting again! I'm absolutely delighted.' Unlike my mother and Jean, she wrote at length. She told me when the baby would be born, what she hoped it would be, what names they fancied, and so forth. The topic bored me and Catriona knew it, and I think that was why she had to keep going on for she was determined that I, in the

60

end, would say that I envied her.

When she had finished with that subject she wrote, 'James has got a new girlfriend! I thought you might like to know. I don't suppose you care anyway since you're finished with him. She's called Charlotte and her father's a doctor and she lives further along Heriot Row. She's going to Edinburgh University next year to study Fine Art. She's got long brown hair down past her shoulders and grey eyes and she's quite pretty.'

So James had found himself another girl. Did I care? No, not really, I couldn't find any jealousy within me, just this deep regret that we had parted so bitterly. I wanted to be able to think about him without that bitterness and it seemed terrible that two people who had been as close as we had at one time could now feel so far apart from one another. A sense of loss filled me.

I took out my notepaper and wrote two letters, one to my folks and the other to Catriona. In both epistles I was cheerful and gave a glowing account of my week in Ottawa, saying nothing at all about homesickness or feelings of loss. I sent congratulations to Catriona and asked her to let me know how James's affair was proceeding with Charlotte. She sounded the very thing for him, a nice girl from a suitable family. Perhaps even Mrs Fraser would approve.

In the morning I was awakened early by Mrs Willoughby cooing at my door: 'Elmer's awake.' It seemed that that was my signal to rise, which I did, grumbling inwardly. Mornings are not my best times, and coping with a three-year-old before I came to properly was not going to be the easiest thing in the world. And this three-year-old was standing in the passage, bare-footed, and in pyjamas, glaring at me.

'Don't like you. Want my mommy.' A good start. As far as I was concerned, he could have had his mommy,

61

but presumably she would not want him. She had swished her silken way back along the corridor and I had heard the door of her bedroom clicking firmly behind her. She paid good money not to be bothered early in the day.

I looked at the child and wondered what to say to him.

He knew what to say to me. 'Want my mommy.' He started to scream.

She did not come, but his brother Roland, the hyper-intelligent one, did. Eyes gleaming behind spectacles, this genius surveyed me, and easily summed up the situation. 'Guess you don't have too much experience with young kids, eh?'

Recalling that it was necessary to assert one's authority right at the beginning or else one would lose ground that would not be recovered, I told him sternly that I was exceedingly experienced, having a younger sister and brother. 'Now come along, both of you, and we'll go down to the kitchen and get some breakfast.'

Neither of them came. When I was half-way along the landing I looked back to see them standing exactly where I'd left them. Elmer had, however, stopped crying and seemed to be interested in what was developing between Roland and me.

'Come on, Roland,' I said firmly.

'I'll be down in half-an-hour,' said Roland, and he disappeared into his bedroom, slamming the door behind him.

The door of Mrs Willoughby's room opened again. She put her hand to her head. 'Really, Margaret, you mustn't let the kids make such a racket this early in the morning. My husband and I have a very heavy day ahead.'

'Sorry,' I said, wondering what kind of day I had ahead, and then, at speed, came back along the landing and grabbed Elmer before he knew what was happening to him. I carried him downstairs, under my arm, whilst he squawked loudly and kicked the back of my legs.

'I'll tell my mommy.'

It seemed an empty threat since she was unlikely to listen. We only saw her briefly before she dashed off to the shop. The housekeeper served our meals, with scarcely a word. She didn't have much English, and didn't seem to be interested in the children. The house was her care. She cleaned and polished it lovingly, sitting back on her heels to admire the gleam on the parquet flooring.

'Mommy loves new clothes,' said Tracey. 'I like them too, do you?'

She seemed astonished when I said I didn't care much one way or the other, that I usually wore jeans. Tracey said that when she grew up she was going to wear pretty clothes every day. She spent most of her time dressing and undressing her large array of dolls, and so was little bother. I couldn't say the same for the two boys. Elmer growled and roared and cried at the slightest excuse, with not too many tears in his eye, urged on and applauded silently by elder brother Roland. It was Roland whom I could cheerfully have strangled, for there he sat with his eyes gleaming behind those glasses observing closely how I mishandled his small brother.

'I wouldn't say you had *too* much knack at dealing with small kids.'

Sharply, I told him not to be so cheeky, for the tenth time. He said solemnly that he was not being cheeky, he was merely passing a remark based on what he saw. I wondered if he could really be ten years old or whether he was an old man masquerading as a child.

'You don't like us too much, do you?' he said, as I served them burnt hamburgers for lunch. The house-keeper was finishing the windows and had asked me to

63

keep an eye on them. Roland seemed pleased with the idea that I might not like them. I told him that he was talking rubbish, but he smiled, examined his hamburger and said that I wasn't too much use as a cook either, was I?

Mrs Willoughby returned home around six-thirty. She fixed herself a Tom Collins in the kitchen and whilst leaning against the counter to drink it asked me how I'd got on that day.

'She burnt the hamburgers,' said Roland.

'She did? Charred food's bad for the stomach.'

'It sure is,' said Roland. 'And then we had some custard and it was all lumpy. Yuck! I don't think it was cooked properly.'

'Maggie never wears nice frocks, Mommy,' said Tracey.

Mrs Willoughby surveyed my jeans. 'As a matter of fact, Margaret, I was going to mention it – I don't think you should wear those dirty jeans when you're working with the kids. Can't you wear a pretty dress or something? The children are used to seeing women nicely dressed.'

I looked down at the offending jeans. Perhaps they were a little scuffed and dirty, for I had worn them for a full week in Ottawa scrambling through woods and sitting on the ground to eat picnics, but, after all, people didn't bother about things like that now, did they? And then I thought, well, she's paying me, isn't she? I said I had a couple of dresses with me and I'd go up and change.

'I bet they're not as nice as my mommy's dresses,' said Tracey.

'Now, Tracey!' said her mother, smiling. She seemed to think that every utterance her children gave forth was divine. Particularly utterances made by her son Roland, the genius.

The genius accompanied me to the bathroom when I bathed Elmer. He leant against the door jamb.

'The last girl we had nearly drowned Elmer.'

It was a pity that she hadn't managed to drown Roland.

'Have you had many girls?'

'About a dozen, I reckon.' He grinned. 'They don't last long.'

Now that I could read him, now that I knew he was trying to rile me so that he could get rid of me, I felt stronger and more able to cope with him. He wouldn't get rid of me, not before I was prepared to go, and that would be the end of the summer when I was due to go back to Scotland. I needed to earn money for three months and this was a good enough job with very good pay. I was determined to stick it out. To stick him out.

'You think you're smart, don't you?' I said, unable to resist a jibe in return, unable to resist, as I knew I should, coming down to his level.

'I sure do. Nothing wrong in being smart. Better than being dumb.'

'You just watch it.'

'Watch what?'

I wrapped Elmer up in a towel and carried him to the nursery, followed once more by my shadow. Perhaps his mother was paying him as a spy to report on my movements. Anything was possible. Mr Willoughby I heard in the distance but did not see, and he was not brought out to be introduced to me. When the children had gone to bed, I went up to my room where I read, wrote letters and watched my little television set. I had a phone call from Phil who rang to see how I was settling in, but it had to be kept short as Mrs Willoughby, when she came to fetch me, asked me to be brief as her husband was waiting for a call from New York. I wondered if that was true or not as I didn't hear the phone ring again afterwards. I thought possibly she wanted to discourage me from spending hours on their telephone.

For the first day or two I suffered a bit from claustrophobia. It was just that I was not used to rich people's houses. I had always thought the Frasers in Edinburgh were pretty well off but their degree of wealth was nothing compared to this. Mrs Willoughby had every kind of gadget imaginable, and many that were not. They had four cars in the garage outside and a woman who came in every day for three hours to clean, apart from the housekeeper, and a man who came daily to do the garden. Roland informed me that his father was a big businessman. He said that he intended to be one too when he grew up. His ambition was to be a millionaire and I did not doubt that he would achieve it.

I took the children two or three times a day to a nearby park where Tracey and Elmer played with a ball and ran about whilst Roland lay on the grass under a tree and read books about space and moon rockets. He was incredibly well informed on both of these topics, and many others. On the walk to and from the park we seldom seemed to pass anyone. These were roads where people did not walk; they came and went to their large houses in swift gleaming cars. I never had any need to go to the shops because Mrs Willoughby ordered all the provisions by phone. I badly missed town streets and shop windows. I felt buried in deepest suburbia, where even the noises were muffled by the thickness of the trees and the solidity of the houses. It was yet another way of life for me to observe, I told myself, with other patterns of behaviour, and quite different again from Mike's family in Ottawa. I certainly couldn't imagine Mrs Willoughby getting into jogging. She took sauna baths and went to a slimming clinic where she had vibro massage and was tanned artificially. She told me it bored her to lie in the sun.

On my fifth day she said to me, 'You seem to be settling in nicely, Margaret?'

I said that I felt I was getting along fairly well with the children. All except Roland, but I didn't add that. She could hardly expect anyone to get along with Roland, she must know that for herself, even if she wouldn't admit it. I had the feeling he was too much even for her; he had already outstripped her intellectually.

'Seeing you're getting along so well with the kids, we thought we might take a little trip to Acapulco.' Acapulco? Mexico? She nodded. She just loved Mexico. When was she thinking of going?

'Tomorrow.'

'Tomorrow?' I echoed, parrot-like.

Her husband had called that morning to say he'd got the reservations, and it just so happened that her sister and husband were going to Acapulco too, at the same time.

'That'll be nice for you,' I said, thinking of myself alone with the three children. Thinking of myself with Roland.

'Yes, it should be real nice.' She hesitated one moment, then said, 'I've been thinking – well, my sister has two kids, they're older than ours, and I think they'd be a good help to you while we're away.'

'Another two kids?'

'They're almost adults. They could give you a hand with our lot. Melanie is thirteen and a real cute girl, and Grant's twelve. You'll just love them. And, anyway, you'll have Mrs—.' She added the housekeeper's name, which I'd still not cottoned on to.

Melanie and Grant came the next morning carrying luggage for a fortnight.

'You've come for two weeks?' I said.

'Sure,' said Melanie. 'Well, they'll be gone for two weeks, won't they? They always go for two weeks. They say it's not worth going for less.'

The housekeeper carried up the children's luggage. Mrs Willoughby bustled around the house packing for herself and her husband of whom I had managed to catch one glimpse as he passed along the corridor. He had nodded to me. He looked as if he was abstracted with the cares of the business world and that the nursery maid was something far below his notice. His wife moved through the house like a whirlwind gathering up possessions, leaving instructions, writing notes, chattering breathlessly. And then they were gone, and I was left alone with the five children, and the silent, house-proud housekeeper.

'You can hardly refer to Grant and me as *children*,' said Melanie. 'I am virtually grown-up after all. Look at me!' She pushed out her chest trying to accentuate the beginnings of a bosom. There wasn't too much there to work on.

'She sure thinks she's great,' said her brother with disgust.

'There's no reason why she shouldn't,' said Roland. 'Everyone is entitled to have a good opinion of himself if he wants to have it.'

I thought it might be a good idea if Roland and Melanie could take themselves off and impress one another with their claims for superiority, and leave me with the other three whom I most definitely preferred. Melanie trailed round the house looking disdainful, and spent long hours in Mrs Willoughby's bedroom trying on her clothes, even after I had told her not to since her aunt would be furious if she came back and found her wardrobe had been touched. Melanie informed me that her aunt would not mind if she touched her things; it would be different if *I* touched them. Often I felt that she was inviting me to slap her but that was something I would not do however much I was tempted. There were times when I had to sit on my hands. Over meals she told me about all the boys at school who admired her.

On the day after the Willoughbys took off for Acapulco Phil rang again. He said he'd tried to call me a couple of times before but I'd not been in. It was the housekeeper who had answered and she hadn't told me. Either she'd forgotten, or more likely, couldn't be bothered. I felt a pang at having missed him. My heartbeat quickened and I felt slightly breathless, silly fool that I was!

'But you're okay, are you? Liking the job?'

'Oh yes, yes indeed,' I said, not wanting to deliver in his ear a list of grievances. I was mindful of the moaning and groaning my family indulged in, and how tedious it was for everybody else. And, after all, Phil and Mike had been good enough to take the trouble to find me the job.

We chatted for almost an hour since Mr Willoughby was not at hand to await calls from New York. Phil told me stories about his job as a lifeguard which made me laugh; he could always see the funny side of things. He had some strange requests from some strange people as he sat in his red track suit on a high stool looking out over the beach. I felt pretty sure that a lot of girls must eye him and even approach him and the thought made me feel jealous. My idiocy appeared to know no bounds! I had no right at all to feel jealous about Phil. That didn't seem to matter however.

'How's Lois?' I asked.

She was fine, she was working in a department store. He seemed not to wish to linger on that topic, and I wasn't sure why I'd brought it up, unless it was that I was secretly hoping that he might have said, very casually, 'Oh, Lois? Oh, we're not seeing one another any more. . . .'

Before ringing off, he promised he'd come over and see me very soon.

I went around the house humming to myself.

'You love-sick or something?' said Roland.

He escaped round the corner before I could come to and retaliate.

My spell of mooniness did not last long, however; it did not get a chance to. I came around the corner of the hall to find the houeskeeper on her knees, bent over, moaning. At first I thought maybe a kid had spilled something on her beautiful shining floor and then I realised that she was in pain. I tried to help her up but the moaning turned to groaning and I saw her face, ashen-coloured, and beaded with sweat. I yelled to Roland to phone the doctor, who came quickly and phoned for an ambulance. She was whisked away to hospital and operated on for appendicitis. She would be in hospital for at least two weeks, for the rest of the time the Willoughbys would be away.

I decided I'd better send them a cablegram.

'No need to do that,' said Melanie. 'We can manage, sure we can! I'll polish the floors.'

I hesitated, and, naturally, was lost.

'Ah come on, Maggie, we don't need a house-keeper. . . .'

I quite liked the idea of being alone with the kids, even though they were a trial: it gave me a feeling of freedom, of being in charge, able to run the show, without anyone looking on. It didn't appeal to me to have Mrs Willoughby return, though I did wonder if she would. I decided I would write, tell her that I was managing, and see what transpired. If things got too hectic I could always phone Acapulco and yell for help, if my stubborn pride would allow me to take such action, which was not too likely. I'd be on my knees before I yelled 'Help!' to Mrs Willoughby.

She rang three days later: she had just received my letter.

'How's it going, Margaret?'

'Fine.'

'Good.' She paused. 'You can cope on your own eh? No need for us to come back?'

No need whatsoever, I informed her, feeling, at that moment, superbly confident and in control, although half an hour before I had been screaming blue murder at Roland who had fifty thousand subtle ways of being annoying.

'Okay?' asked Roland, who had been loitering in the background.

'Okay.'

'There's a guy here looking for you,' said Melanie, leading Phil into the room.

'Phil!'

'Hi, Maggie!'

We stood and stared at one another, kind of daft like. Then I noticed that all the kids had joined us.

'Do you play baseball?' Grant asked of Phil, who admitted that he did, pretty well too. 'Yeah? Want a game?'

We all fancied a game, even I, who have never been noted for an addiction to sport. But today I felt like exercise in the fresh air: I needed physical action.

On the way to the park, with the children running ahead carrying the gear, Phil said to me, after some throat-clearing, 'Did you get my last letter, Maggie?'

'Oh, your letter? Yes, sure.' I hoped I sounded casual, even nonchalant.

'I didn't know—'

'Forget it! Anyway, I wasn't coming to Canada just. . . .' I trailed off too now. I had been going to add, 'because of you', but I couldn't quite get it out, and it might have sounded too cool. We were both at a loss so I decided in my usual ostrich-like way, whenever a situation is tricky, that it's better to pretend there's nothing to discuss. 'It's nice we can still be friends. Come on, let's catch the kids!'

We had a great afternoon. I wouldn't say I excelled exactly in the art of baseball: I missed nearly everything I was supposed to catch and every time I had the bat in my hands the ball had a nasty habit of passing it by a half-inch. It had the effect of sending the kids into convulsions of delight for I usually ended up almost laying myself out, so vigorously did I wield the bat. Once or twice Phil also collapsed laughing, saying, 'Really, Maggie!' He was the life and soul of the outing, organising us all, goading us to greater effort, cheering our successes. He was never still for a minute, ran hither and thither with seemingly unflaggable energy. At half-time I subsided into a heap on the grass.

He joined me, so did Elmer, and then Tracey. The other three arrived. Flies round the honey pot. Tracey sat on Phil's knee and put her arm around his neck.

'We'll make a baseball player of you yet, Maggie,' said Phil.

'It'd be okay as long as she played on the opposite team,' said Roland.

'Thank you, Roland,' I said, quite unriled. I lay back, letting my head rest on the brittle dry grass. The sky was very blue with scarcely a wisp of cloud. I was happy.

But we weren't going to be allowed to laze for long like this, no sir! Come on, on your dying feet! Phil yanked me up. Such energy the boy had!

I expect my team must have lost, I don't remember. It was of no importance. We walked home at the end of the afternoon in single file with Phil leading the way carrying Elmer on his shoulders and me bringing up the rear carrying most of the clobber. We sang, 'When the saints go marching in,' shattering the suburban peace, even Roland, whom I'd never have imagined would indulge in such undignified behaviour.

'It's just as well Aunt Betty's away in Mexico,' giggled Melanie.

We had long iced-lemon drinks in the back garden and recovered from our exertions. I wondered how long Phil planned to stay. Was he working today? I asked and he shook his head.

'Want to stay to supper?'

'Love to. Say, have you got a barbecue? I'm a whiz at barbecuing.'

Of course they had a barbecue. What a question! We had kebabs prepared à la McKinley (I managed to do a good job of piercing my fingers as well as the tomatoes and bits of meat and whatnot) and cooked by Phil. They tasted delicious. Then we had ice-cream and mangoes and nuts and cheesecake. . . .

'That's enough, Melanie,' I said. 'No more! We'll all burst.'

I put the two young ones to bed without bathing them and the rest of us sat in the kitchen and drank coke. And Melanie stacked up the dishwasher. Miraculous!

'You performed a miracle with those kids,' I told Phil when they had gone up to bed. I had never seen them so nice, so uncomplaining, so positive.

He grinned. 'I'm a novelty, that's all.'

He lingered. We talked until midnight, about all sorts of things, geology and history, politics, Scotland and Canada. We discussed Scottish devolution and French separatism. We didn't talk about him and me. I'd had my chance to do that earlier and hadn't taken it.

We said goodnight on the doorstep.

'Thanks, Maggie, it's been great.'

'Thank *you* for coming.'

'You're welcome!' He hesitated a moment. 'I'll see you.'

I nodded. 'Goodnight, Phil.'

I waited in the porch until he drove away. The night smelled fragrant. I stood there drinking it in until I suddenly realised I was being eaten by my least favourite insects. Hurriedly, I retreated.

In the morning we were all restless, or so it seemed. Perhaps it was that Phil's visit had brought in a whiff of the outside world, a refreshing, invigorating whiff, and we were loath to let it go.

'Let's do something interesting today,' said Melanie over breakfast. 'I'm bored with this stuffy old house.'

'I second that,' said Roland, 'although the house is not old or stuffy! But it's about time we made an expedition.'

'Let's go to Ontario Place,' suggested Melanie. 'It's great fun.' She told me that it was an island that had been made on Lake Ontario and it boasted all sorts of amusements, experimental theatres, a children's village, marina, mini golf course, restaurants and boutiques, and many other things.

I agreed at once. Led by Melanie, we set off, and went there taking a series of street cars and buses. She evidently knew her way around the city, although Roland was not allowed to go out on his own, in spite of his intelligence. He said that his mother didn't have enough confidence in herself, otherwise she would let him go alone, for he knew perfectly well that he was capable of getting anywhere he wanted and home again.

Ontario Place was crowded but, as Melanie had said, there were lots of amusements and plenty of space. I felt excitement spring up in me. 'Stay close to me now,' I told the children. 'We mustn't get separated.'

Melanie objected. She said that they couldn't stick around doing what Elmer wanted to do all day, so she suggested that I went with Tracey and Elmer to the children's village and that the three of them, the older ones, could go around together. 'We can meet you back at the children's village. Okay?'

She was not actually asking for my permission, but I gave it anyway. It was a reasonable proposition. I took the two little ones and set off for the children's play area. There were slides and ropes and contraptions to bounce up and down on and jump over, things that would keep them happy for hours.

'Look after Elmer for me, Tracey,' I told her. 'I'll sit and watch you from the side.'

Tracey took her brother by the hand and led him off to the climbing ropes. There were attendants around, girls and boys of about my own age who looked like high school students doing summer jobs. This was a good idea, I decided, as I sat on a step with my back to the sun, feeling the warmth penetrate my bones. It was a relief to be in a place where there were a lot of people around, and not to walk through muffled, silent streets. From the mêlée of kids playing in front of me I could hear the laughter of Tracey and Elmer rising up. It was amazing how you were able to pick out your own kids' voices and laughter from so many. Then I saw Tracey take Elmer by the hand again and they began to run in and out of large coloured sandbags suspended from rods. They shrieked as the bags swung to and fro hitting them lightly in the face.

The day was warm and pleasant, the kids were happy and occupied. There was one thing wrong – the absence of Phil. I wished that he was here with me – no, it was stronger than that, I longed for him to be here – and then we too could have laughed and run in amongst the sandbags after the children. I sat and hugged my knees and thought about his dark eyes that were so full of life.

And I thought of how he looked at me directly when he spoke to me. And I thought of the way he smiled, with all of his face lighting up, not just his mouth. I liked his energy and vitality and his enthusiasm. When he talked about stones and rock formations I wanted to be a geologist too. I sighed. For heaven's sake, McKinley, quit it or you'll be dripping tears all over Ontario Place! But I couldn't quit it, I couldn't stop thinking about him.

Sitting there, I faced up to it: I was in love with Phil Ross. And then I tried to face up to the next thought, which was that my love was unrequited. Obviously. Well, he had Lois, hadn't he? I, Maggie McKinley, was suffering from unrequited love, and not finding it a particularly enjoyable experience. James Fraser might not be one bit sorry if he could see me now; he might say grimly that it served me right, it might make me understand what he had been through. I felt twisted inside when I thought of him and how he had suffered because of me.

Following on came another thought, equally unpleasant. Was I perverse, in that I could only be in love with a boy if he didn't want me? I could have had James, I could have had Mike, and I hadn't wanted either in the end, although I had, I reminded myself, wanted James for one year. Sternly I admonished myself, reflecting that no good would come from this morbid introspection. Better to take up that ostrich position again. James had often accused me of burying my head in the sand when something emotional was pressing. But the sand seemed to be shallow where I was now, almost non-existent. Where could I put my head at all?

Mrs Fraser came to see me on the evening after James and I had our final quarrel.

'Maggie,' she said, 'I'd like to have a wee talk with you.'

I didn't feel like wee talks, I'd had them before with Mrs Fraser and they had always been on one topic. James. But I went: it was easier than not to go. She always banked on that.

We walked down through the village, past the closed shops. There were a few tourists hanging about not knowing how to fill their evening.

'You know I'm very fond of you, Maggie.' She paused, to gather strength. I like the way that people say they're fond of you just before they prepare to stab you, either in the front or the back. But, to be honest to Mrs Fraser, I knew she would stab me only in the front. 'I must speak plainly to you. You know I always believe in plain speaking. And what I want to say to you is this, Maggie: I think you've played around with James long enough and it's time you left him to get on with his life. I know you probably didn't mean to hurt him—'

'Of course I didn't!'

She softened her voice a little. Patiently, she said that she was sure I hadn't wanted to hurt him but I could not deny that I had, and more than once?

It didn't seem worth the bother to try to explain or excuse myself. I said stiffly that I had finished with James for once and for all, and that I did not intend to see him again. From the look on Mrs Fraser's face I could see that she hoped not to see me again either. And although I did not care too much about that again I was saddened, by the idea that I had lost the friendship of the Fraser family. They had enlivened many of my summer days in the glen, and, in a funny way, I would miss even Mrs Fraser herself. The only one whose friendship I could count on would be Catriona's.

I realised that night, when I lay awake, that I had lost

not only my granny but a whole area of my life: her wild and beautiful glen. I wouldn't be able to stay with the Frasers any more and my granny's flat would be rented out to some other old person. The glen would be there of course and no one could prevent me walking the narrow twisting road or climbing the heather- and bracken-covered hills, but it would no longer be a place I would come to regularly and so would cease to be an integral part of my life.

I sighed, once more. How destructive love could be, at least in its ending!

And why on earth should I be dwelling on such miserable thoughts on such a warm, happy day, when kids all around me were having a good time and filling the air with laughter? Thinking of kids and laughter, I stood up and scanned the small moving figures. I thought I saw a familiar blonde head bobbing in and out of the sandbags.

'Tracey!'

She came to me, dodging between two bags. She began rattling out a list of all the things she'd done.

'Where's Elmer?' I interrupted her.

'Elmer?'

Her brother, silly! Where was he? Had she let go of his hand? Her face crumpled and she nodded. In her excitement and enjoyment, she had obviously forgotten her small brother.

'I expect he's around,' I muttered, a trifle uneasy, taking Tracey's hand into mine, determined not to lose her as well. Of course I hadn't lost Elmer! He would probably be sitting a few yards away playing with something that had taken his fancy. 'Come on then, let's go find him.'

We searched every piece of apparatus, every corner of

the children's village, two or three times over, but there was no sign at all of him. We called out his name, repeatedly, but no answering call came back. Tracey began to cry.

Chapter 5

'Now don't cry, Tracey, he must be around somewhere. We'll go and ask the attendants to help us find him.'

We found a girl and gave a full description of our lost child. Three years old, curly blond hair, blue eyes, inclined to suck his thumb when troubled, answering to the name of Elmer. I imagined him sucking his thumb at this moment, wandering amongst the tall legs of jostling people.

The attendant was cheerful, said that kids were lost all the time, and usually found again. Usually? Always! She said I'd soon see, someone would come along any minute now leading him by the hand. Even as we spoke one other small boy was brought in: a dark-haired boy wearing a red striped T-shirt and crying noisily. He sobbed and sobbed but eventually the girl calmed him down and he said his name was Bill.

'Sit here, Bill, and I'll see if I can find you some candy.'

'Will Elmer get candy?' asked Tracey, drying her tears. 'Will he share it with me? I bet he won't!'

I promised to buy her some, and an ice-cream. I would have promised her anything, if it would have brought Elmer back. We went to sit on the step where I had sat before dwelling on my misery and thus taken my eyes off my charges.

As we sat down the other three returned, Roland

leading the way sucking a large ice-cream.

'We've lost Elmer,' bleated Tracey at once, her eyes shining with excitement. She enjoyed giving the news to Roland, I could see that.

'Lost Elmer? Gee, Mom won't be pleased at that.'

I retorted that I fully expected to find him again, that I didn't think he was lost for ever. How come he had wandered and I hadn't noticed? asked Roland.

'It's none of your business!'

'It sure is. He's my brother, isn't he? You can't deny that he's my brother?'

I didn't deny it. I didn't answer. My eyes were scurrying to and fro examining every small child around the height of Elmer. Tracey began to whine so I gave Melanie money for ice-creams. They would need large ones, declared Roland; they might have a long wait. I let Melanie go, made the rest stay close beside me. I was even loath to let her out of my sight but I reckoned that a thirteen-year-old girl couldn't very easily get lost. Unless she was trying to, of course.

'Perhaps somebody has kidnapped him,' said Roland.

'Don't be silly! What would anyone want to kidnap him for?' I should have known better than to enter into any discussion about that at all.

Solemnly, slipping his tongue around the edge of his ice-cream cone, Roland said, 'For money of course.' His father was rich.

Not all that rich, I replied. This Roland contested, telling me how much their house was worth, how much the cars were worth, and so on. I told him I wasn't interested in a catalogue of his family's wealth.

'But the kidnapper obviously is.'

Tracey began to cry. I told her not to listen to Roland and I told Roland to shut up. He wasn't helping at all.

'We have to consider all the possibilities.'

81

'How would anyone know that Elmer's father had any money?'

I began to scratch my arms and legs, especially in the areas where I had been well bitten by my old friends the mosquitoes. Some of the lumps had scabs on them. Roland was watching me with interest, letting his eyes slide up and down my arms and legs as my hands moved up and down them.

'You shouldn't scratch mosquito bites,' he said, taking another lick. 'You'll only make them worse.'

I stood up, shading my eyes against the sun with my hand. Roland, below me, observed that that wouldn't bring Elmer any faster. I ordered him to stay where he was, beside the other two, and I went down to speak to the attendant again. She shrugged. No one had come up with a three-year-old blond boy yet, she said, but it was too early to give up hope, far too early. Sometimes it took an hour or two; it was quite amazing where the kids wandered. The island was so large and so diverse that it wasn't possible to start searching the whole place thoroughly, at least not at the moment. If he didn't turn up in two or three hours well then.... Two or three hours!

I returned to the children. Melanie had come back with the ice-creams and they were all licking and slurping happily. She had brought one for me too, but the very thought of taking even a mouthful made me feel sick. It was bright green. Roland said that he could manage it and so he sat with one large cone in each hand. I couldn't sit, couldn't settle; I had to be on the move. The five of them should stay where they were, I stressed, not move an inch in any direction, and I would go and take a look around. I put Melanie in charge.

I looked in the area where kids were playing with water. No sign of him there. On I went to the mini golf course, where they were playing a kind of crazy golf.

There was no one nearly as small as he was. I searched the different areas of the amusement park, around the sides of the hot-dog and ice-cream stands, went into the shops and boutiques, even glanced inside and behind the wastepaper baskets. Several times I thought I saw him: I rushed forward only to fall back, my hopes deflated, as I looked into the face of a strange little boy. What if someone had kidnapped Elmer? I supposed it was not impossible, that even if he had not been taken away for money he might have been abducted because he was a nice-looking little boy, which he was. He had blond curls and big blue eyes. I began to sweat at the prospect. And it was all my fault, I was under no illusions about that: Elmer was lost because I had allowed myself to drown in a welter of self-pity. I had made a real meal out of my misery. My granny had always warned me against doing that, she had said many times that it was better to be up and doing. And I should never have entrusted Elmer to Tracey, who was only six years old and whose mind was easily distracted.

The island ran off in limbs in all directions: it was clearly impossible for me to search every avenue thoroughly on my own. I went slowly back to where my group were waiting, licking up the last bits of ice-cream.

'He hasn't come back yet,' reported Roland, almost in triumph, I fancied. Clearly he was enjoying the drama, even if no one else was. For a second I wondered if he might have contrived his brother's disappearance. I wouldn't have put it past him. And then I reminded myself that he was only ten, that he was not quite a devil, only an incredible, revolting nuisance.

'I'm still hungry,' he said.

'Well, you can just starve,' I snapped. 'You aren't getting anything else right now.'

One hour passed, and then two. In desperation I went

for the sixth time to speak to the attendants and this time even they were prepared to admit that it was looking rather serious, that lost kids usually reappeared within an hour. The small dark boy who had been sobbing had been claimed and was gone. At present they had a little girl of about five with a pretty red ribbon in her hair; she seemed to be enjoying herself and was sitting on a stool eating a toffee apple.

'Maybe we'll need to go find a policeman soon,' said the girl attendant.

When three hours had passed we found a policeman and a search was organised.

Elmer was found in a men's washroom over by the marina. He had been playing happily in a basin of water, soaked to the skin. And when we questioned him it seemed that he had been there all the time. I asked him if anyone had taken him there and he shook his head. He seemed undisturbed. I was exhausted, drained of energy, wanting only to fall into a deep, deep sleep. With all the other kids protesting, I led them out of Ontario Place and headed for the bus stop.

'We didn't have time to do hardly anything,' said Roland. 'It wasn't fair! I wanted to play miniature golf.'

I didn't answer, I led the way with Tracey firmly gripped by my left hand and Elmer by my right. The other three older ones trailed behind, scuffing their feet, grumping and grousing. What a lovely way to spend a day! I agreed heartily.

There was an enormous queue at the bus stop and we had to wait for ages. Then we had to change on to a street car and we had to wait for that, standing on the sidewalk in the hot sun. Melanie kept saying she was sure she was going to faint. I looked down at Tracey and Elmer's heads, thinking that I should have put sun hats on them. I felt completely irresponsible, and incapable of taking care of small children.

Eventually, a street car with room in it for us arrived, and we clambered aboard.

I fed the two younger children as soon as we got in, bathed them and put them to bed. When I had done that I could have gone to my own bed, but the older ones were still up playing Monopoly and quarrelling like crazy. I could hear Roland's voice shrieking above the other two; he hated to be beaten and would cheat like mad rather than let anyone get the better of him. I stood by the door of the dim bedroom until the two children slept. It seemed necessary for me to see them actually asleep, so that I would know that they were both safe at least until morning.

The I went into my own room, shut the door and burst into tears. They passed quickly; I blew my nose and dried my eyes. But I still felt shaken up and in need of someone to talk to, someone other than Roland or his cousins. I needed to talk to an adult. I needed to talk to Phil.

With trembling fingers, I dialled his number. As I waited for someone to answer I felt sure that he would not be in, that the phone would go on and on ringing in his empty room. But no, someone was lifting the receiver, someone was answering, and it was Phil. I told him my story and he said he would come straight over.

He did, with Lois.

'Hi, Maggie!' said Lois. 'You've had a real bad day, I hear?'

'Phil!' shrieked Melanie, tumbling down the stairs. 'Want a game of Monopoly?'

'Not right at the moment, thanks, Melanie.'

'Ah, come on!' Melanie took hold of him and tried to drag him away.

'Seems like Phil's made a hit there,' said Lois. 'Popular guy, eh?'

I told Melanie sharply that it was time for bed but it was Phil who persuaded her to go telling her he'd come back another day for a game of Monopoly or baseball. I wanted to tell him he needn't bother. I felt frozen-lipped now and shrivelled inside and had no desire to talk to anybody.

We went to the kitchen and I made coffee.

'You know, it can happen to anyone, Maggie,' said Phil.

'What?'

'Why . . . losing kids, of course.'

Lois was smoking a cigarette and watching me from behind the smoke.

Kids were lost all the time, said Phil, and found again; he knew that from his job as a lifeguard. 'You mustn't blame yourself too much, Maggie.' But I did, although I could not tell him why. I could not tell him anything. I sat virtually silent at the other side of the table whilst Lois made comments on the kitchen. She had never seen such a fabulous kitchen.

'Real ritzy house. Mind if I take a peep at a couple of the other rooms?'

She took herself off to peep. Phil looked at me. 'You didn't mind me bringing Lois?'

'Course not.'

'It was just that she was there when you phoned—'

I told him I'd expected him to bring her. Liar!

'What a place!' said Lois, returning. 'Real cool eh?'

I shrugged. Wouldn't do for me. No? Give her the chance and she'd jump at it. She liked the idea of a bit of luxury in life. I felt rather pleased to hear that since I thought it unlikely Phil would aspire to luxury.

They stayed a couple of hours. The conversation was desultory, unlike that of the evening before. They were slightly edgy with one another, I thought, or was it my imagination willing them to be so? But they did seem to contradict one another quite a lot and to be unwilling to let the other get away with anything, particularly Lois, who kept saying, 'Come off it, Phil, you know that's not right.' Whenever I looked her way she seemed to be looking at me in a kind of appraising way. Did she suspect how I felt about Phil? How could she since we'd only spent that one night together previously? Or had he talked about me to her? My head buzzed with speculation.

When they left Phil said if I needed anything anytime I'd only to call. I knew I would not call again. Lois gave me a small smile. She knows! I thought. Part of me was pleased though I wasn't sure why.

Phil called me up on the telephone the next day to see how I was. Great, I told him, just great. We were staying at home today, not even venturing as far as the park. He laughed. He said he'd be around the first chance he got to have that return baseball match but he didn't appear so I guessed that Lois must have taken care of his days off. They came together one evening bringing some beer, and we barbecued Wieners in the garden with the kids. The children monopolised Phil so Lois and I were left to converse uneasily together. There was friction between us, without doubt; I could sense the bad vibrations travelling between us, though we didn't say one nasty word to each other. If anything, we were over-polite. Everything we said was superficial; underneath ran currents of thought which we would have liked to express. I couldn't understand it from her point of view: she had nothing to fear from me. How could she?

We went on no other expeditions whilst the Willoughbys were absent in Acapulco. Daily, over his breakfast cereal, Roland nagged me, proposing further visits to Ontario Place, the Science Museum, the

Planetarium, or the zoo. Firmly I resisted. I was running no further risks, certainly not. It was the park for us, and no further. I could not prevent Melanie from taking the street car into town but I could and did prevent Roland. Glossy postcards came from Acapulco telling the children that the weather was fine, the water warm, and they were all having a lovely, lovely time, and hoped that they, the children, were being good.

'Huh!' said Roland, for once echoing my thoughts.

The day before the Willoughbys were due to return, the house buzzed with speculation. What would they bring back? Tracey wanted a doll and Roland so many things I couldn't keep track of them. I told him he had too much as it was already, that he was selfish and materialistic. My opinion of him, good or bad, didn't upset him for a second. Half of the time I could not guess what went on inside his narrow little head. I imagined that when he grew up he would be either an exceedingly wealthy businessman, or a criminal.

I did my best to clean up the house which was looking somewhat shambolic without the housekeeper's tender loving care. She'd have wept if she could have seen her parquet floors all scuffed and dirty. Melanie had not kept her word. And the daily woman had become laxer and laxer with each day that passed. I was a non-starter as a task-master.

Mr and Mrs Willoughby arrived in the early morning, having flown in via Houston, Texas. We were awakened by the sound of their taxi at the door and came down the stairs to meet them tying our dressing-gown cords as we came. Elmer hung back, clutching my hand. After only two weeks he seemed a little unsure of his mother. I had to admit that I felt kind of pleased to feel his soft warm hand curled into mine, to know that he trusted me, even though I had managed to lose him for three hours at Ontario Place!

'Well, guys, how are you all then?' Mrs Willoughby sailed in, tanned a deep mahogany colour, smelling of expensive perfume. She said that Acapulco had been absolutely great and that when they were older she was going to take them there.

'Promise?' said Roland.

She promised, ever so sweetly. Mr Willoughby was smiling, though he said he was tired and meant to go up and get some rest. He would leave his wife to distribute the presents, which she did, kneeling on the sitting-room floor with the children gathered round her. She had brought me a nice little leather wristband for which I thanked her nicely and then I went upstairs, leaving her alone with her offspring.

They were liberally endowed with presents when they came up to show them to me. Look at this, and this, and this! I remembered my mother and father coming back from a week at Scarborough or Dunoon and bringing us a stick of rock apiece. Not that I cared about that! I certainly wasn't envious of these children, not at all. I knew that within days, possibly hours, half of the objects would be broken and strewn around the nursery floor. Tracey had so many dolls that she didn't know what to do with them, except from time to time when she put on a display round the room. And once she had done that she lost interest.

Mr and Mrs Willoughby dozed the morning away, recovering from the effects of their overnight flight. Melanie and her brother went home, and I took the other three children for a walk so that the house would be quiet.

Mrs Willoughby joined us for lunch in the kitchen. At least she poured herself a Martini and lit a cigarette and sat beside us whilst we ate.

'My God, what a state the house is in, Margaret!'

'I know, but I couldn't help—'

'It's okay, it's okay.' But she didn't sound too convincing.

'And have you been good then, kids?'

'Yes,' said Tracey, 'very good.'

'Good,' repeated Elmer.

Roland swung his legs to and fro under the table. I did not like the look on his face.

'And what have you been doing then?' asked their mother.

'Played ball,' said Tracey. 'Went to the park.'

'Park,' repeated Elmer.

'We went to Ontario Place,' said Roland, and I liked the look on his face even less now.

'Ontario Place!' declared Mrs Willoughby, stubbing out the butt of her cigarette. She turned to me. 'Why did you take them there, Margaret?'

'The children wanted to go.'

'The children want to do a lot of things but I don't let them. They know perfectly well I wouldn't let them go to a place like that.'

I did not dare to ask why not, presuming that she would consider it too vulgar or something. I eyed Roland and wished that I was alone with him.

'We were there nearly all day,' said Roland. 'It was very interesting. Full of people. Crowds and crowds of people.'

Gleefully, Tracey began to describe the sandbags and the climbing ropes and the water hoses. Mrs Willoughby said again that she did not care for them to go to such places and that I must never, never take them there again. I apologised, saying that I had had no idea she would object, and that Melanie had suggested it.

Melanie! She would. Mrs Willoughby pursed her lips. Her sister was going to have her hands full with that one.

Roland finished his glass of milk, rather noisily, and set it on the table with a plonk. 'You'll never guess what happened, Mom? We lost Elmer.'

'You *lost* Elmer?' Her voice rose, clear and sharp.

I jumped in. 'But we found him again.' Well, the proof was there, wasn't it, sitting at the table right beside me, pulling one of his new Mexican toys to bits? He looked up at the sound of his name and his blue eyes opened wider, but he said nothing.

'He was lost for *three* hours,' said Roland.

'Three hours! My God!'

'Everybody was looking for him,' continued Roland. 'The police—'

'The police? For heaven's sake! My baby!' She jumped up and grabbed him to her bosom, making him squawk as he dropped the remains of his toy. She hugged him against her, rocking him. Her eyes were full of fear over the top of his curly golden head, fear that she might have lost him, could easily have lost him.

'He was found in the men's washroom,' said Roland. 'Miles away from where he'd left us.'

Mrs Willoughby's eyes dilated from Roland and then over to me. They stopped to rest on me.

'Some guy must have taken him there,' said Roland.

Now her eyes were bulging, with hatred, for me. How come I had let Elmer get lost? she demanded. How come? It wasn't too much to ask, was it, that I should keep my eyes on a three-year-old and a six-year-old? And I had had the other three kids with me to help as well.

Spluttering, I tried to defend myself, but didn't get the chance. She had but one thought in her mind and that was that she might have lost her baby, and I was the person responsible. I could not deny that, had not, even to myself. When I could get a word in I said that it wasn't all that unusual for children to get lost and so forth, repeating Phil's words. But she wasn't concerned as to whether it was usual or unusual: her children were unique and were not allowed to get lost. She paid out good money to see that they wouldn't get lost, didn't she? Her voice continued to rise, taking on an edge of hysteria. Perhaps she too was beginning to feel a bit guilty, thinking that she had been away in Mexico lying in the sun, whilst back home her children had been taking risks. Strange how often people seem to feel guilt, in all sorts of funny complex ways. But I did feel at that moment that I could understand her, and so let her go on for a bit without attempting to interrupt. Elmer wriggled, wanting to release himself, but she would not let go. She had to hold him firmly against her, to reassure herself that he was here and not still left in some men's washroom back in Ontario Place.

Roland poured himself another glass of milk and was sipping it slowly, like a cat who has found a large bowl of fresh cream.

'I'm terribly sorry, Mrs Willoughby. I can't say any more.'

'I shouldn't think you could! It's all right for you to feel sorry, you should have been more responsible.'

'She left Tracey to look after him,' said Roland.

'Be quiet, Roland!' I said, unable to restrain myself in his direction any longer.

Roland looked up at his mother, enquiringly and innocently.

'Why should he be quiet?' demanded Mrs Willoughby. 'If it weren't for Roland I wouldn't have gotten to know that any of this had happened. It's just as well I can rely on someone.'

Meekly, Roland looked down at his glass of milk, accepting the compliment.

'Mrs Willoughby, Roland's a real troublemaker, and

you must know it!'

That was it! She just about hit the ceiling. How dare I say that her precious Roland was a troublemaker?

The temptation to speak my mind had become too much for me and now that I had tasted blood, as it were – got out my remark about Roland – I could not stop. Not to be able to hold my tongue was one of my faults, according to my mother, one that I admitted to and fought, on and off. This became an 'off' time. I let loose at Mrs Willoughby. I told her what I thought of her as a mother, what I thought of her ingratitude (hadn't I coped with five children all on my own with no housekeeper?), of her lack of fairness, her selfishness, her smallmindedness. I even used the word pusillanimity. That would have made Mr Scott smile! I could have run on for hours I was so thoroughly worked up and into the swing of it, whilst at the same time being in control of myself. I spoke strongly but not emotionally, which I knew gave me an emotional advantage. It might not have been very admirable – and I'm not claiming that it was – but I was enjoying myself and the more goggle-eyed she became the more I wanted to continue my diatribe. Also, it was a great release, and no doubt I was working out a few frustrations on poor Mrs Willoughby. Yes, poor Mrs Willoughby, for that was how I couldn't help seeing her afterwards. I didn't envy her life one bit although I don't suppose she'd have wanted it any other way. Finally I informed her what she could do with her job and her precious children.

My speech was interrupted by the arrival of Mr Willoughby. 'What the hell's going on here?' he demanded.

'I am merely handing in my notice to Mrs Willoughby,' I said, very coldly, and added that I had never been so inconsiderately treated in any other employment

93

in my life. I intended to leave immediately. I swept past them, up the stairs, to pack, feeling as an actress must on leaving the stage after an intensely dramatic scene. One in which she has left the audience slightly stunned.

Humming, I threw my belongings together, bundling the last bits into whatever carrier bags I could lay hands on.

Mr Willoughby paid me two weeks' wages, my legal due. Mrs Willoughby I did not see: she had gone to lie down. She had a headache. The children came to say goodbye, even Roland. Was that gleam in his eye respect? I rather fancied that it might be.

Somewhat intoxicated, I staggered through the leafy quiet streets to the subway, dragging my suitcases and bags, some of which came apart en route and had to be repacked. But I didn't care, not one bit! For wasn't I shot of Mrs Willoughby and her plushy prison and her genius of a son Roland?

Chapter 6

The Toronto subway is clean and fast and efficient, too fast for me on that particular occasion, for before I knew it or could think any further, I had arrived at the downtown stop where I planned to get off. Gathering up my bundles, I just made it through the fast-shutting doors on to the platform. I almost had to leave my last paper bag behind.

Up the escalator I went, out into the street. I had an idea where I could locate the Tourist Office, which was where I was heading, to ask them if they knew where I could find some cheapish hotel accommodation. The girl was sympathetic, understood that my money was limited, and came up with a couple of suggestions. She asked if I'd like her to phone and see if they had a room. She did, and they had. It was about twenty minutes' walk, or five minutes on the subway and five minutes' walk from there.

Since I couldn't face going back down on the escalator again dropping my rubbish, and then trying to squeeze in through those doors which threatened to shut on me like a pair of jaws, I elected to walk. Every few yards I dropped something, needless to say, and many passers-by were helpful. 'Thank you,' I said, as I gratefully received dropped objects. 'Can you manage?' 'Oh yes, fine. Thanks very much.' In that way I progressed along the streets, taking forty minutes instead of twenty, and came eventually to the hotel where I was to stay the night.

The clerk at the reception sniffed, eyeing my bits and pieces. 'You Miss McKinley? Miss Margaret McKinley?' I admitted that it was I, and no one else. He continued to eye me with some suspicion.

With a flourish I signed my name in the register and he gave me the key of my room. 'Need any help?' he asked, not budging one inch from his stool. This was not one of those snazzy hotels full of porters and bellhops in decorated uniforms ready to snatch your luggage at the snap of your fingers. I piled my gear into the elevator and sailed up to my room.

The room was okay, it would do well enough for a night or two. That would be as much as I would be able to afford for although it was not expensive, by Toronto standards, it was for me. It was, in fact, the very first time I had ever stayed in a hotel. My family's holidays had never extended to more than a week in a caravan at Dunoon or Rothesay, or a chalet near Scarborough.

I examined the room, which didn't take long. A bed, wardrobe, dressing table, an easy chair which didn't look very easy, and that was about it. But there was a telephone on the small table beside the bed, which pleased me. It was a link. To whom? I could always phone home, to Glasgow, and reverse the charges. I grinned at the thought of my mother's face if I were to reverse the charges from Toronto to Glasgow. She'd need smelling salts to revive her.

There was not much to see out of the window, except for the backs of other buildings. I would have preferred to have been on the front street, where I could have looked down and watched the traffic pass below. I was on the fifth floor. This was no skyscraper hotel like some further down town which soared upwards for about forty floors.

I lay down on the bed to recover from my exertions and

96

before I knew it had drifted into sleep. It had been a pretty exhausting day.

When I awoke the room was in dusk. I jerked up, not knowing for a moment where I was. And then it all came back to me. I began to laugh, out loud, remembering Roland and Mrs Willoughby, and I was very very happy to be rid of them, all of them, except for perhaps little Elmer of whom I had grown quite fond.

My tummy rumbled, reminding me that I had not eaten for hours. I got up, washed my face and tugged a comb through my hair and went out into the streets of Toronto. I bought a hot dog and ate it whilst I walked.

I was alone in a relatively strange city thousands of miles from home. I was elated. I felt cool, sophisticated, and wordly-wise. All the things I had ever wanted to be. They seemed easier to achieve here than back home in my native Glasgow, where I would only need to turn a corner and bump into someone who had known me for years and would say, 'Oh, hullo there, Maggie, how are you doing, hen?' No one here was likely to stop and call me hen.

The city was busy, and the closer to the centre I got, and the thicker the traffic and the crowds got, the more I felt myself becoming truly alive. It was as if the world was outlined more sharply than ever before, just as the glen had been on the day of my granny's funeral. Every part of me was aware; I was aware of the lights, the people, the noise, the ceaseless movement. I felt the pulse of the city. I wanted to skip, to dance, to sing. How I hated the suburbs, especially the rich cloying suburbs, and how unimportant and far away they were from me now! It was difficult to believe in their existence, to believe in the existence of people like Mrs Willoughby. As far as I was concerned they were dead, dead, dead.

'Dead, dead, dead,' I sang softly to myself, causing two heads to turn, four eyes to stare back at me. I smiled at them and passed on.

I felt intoxicated by the city, by the idea of being alive, by the idea of being alive and alone in the city. Nothing was closed to me. Nothing was impossible.

There were shops open selling books and records, hamburgers and clothes, oriental and occidental. Into some I went, to look and to mingle. For ninety-nine cents you could have a T-shirt with almost any pattern on it that you liked. You could have a maple leaf or a beaver on your chest, Cooky Monster, or Scottish Power. At a rack showing T-shirts of Scottish Power I stopped. The emblem was a clenched fist with a tartan surround. I shivered, my intoxication broken for a moment. Clenched fists did not appeal, the symbol was for real, with no humour intended. It made me afraid for Scotland.

Sam the Record Man's was packed with teenagers and post-teenagers in denim. I mingled, anonymous, wanting to be a part of the crowd. I felt so free!

On, out again, into the night streets I went.

'Topless All Day', said the sign. I had seen several notices like that. Imagine it! What a way to earn your living! Men were pouring in to see the topless girls whom I pitied though I knew they would have been scornful of my pity. No slave labour now, you know, chum! Women had a choice more than ever before in their lives. And did I know it! My mother had never had as much choice as I, still less my granny. At the thought of her my steps slowed a little; she had never trod any city streets in her life but had lived in an unilluminated glen uncontaminated by neon signs of commercial establishments. Strange that she and I, so different by inclination, enjoying such different aspects of life, should have felt so close. Kindred spirits: that was the only way I could describe it.

Get on, lassie, enjoy yoursel' and quit havering!

I glanced over my shoulder, imagining that she had spoken. I looked into the face of a Japanese girl and almost tripped her up. The words had certainly not come from her lips.

Obediently, I went on and gave over havering. The evening, with all that it had to offer, was too demanding. I passed cafés, bars, places of entertainment. I liked them to be there even though I might not go into them. I moved onward, part of a moving tide.

Eventually, hunger began to gnaw again, for the hot dog had only filled a small corner. I selected a café, a steakhouse, and ordered a steak with salad and French fries. My mouth watered whilst I waited. I wanted nothing more at that moment than to be awaiting a good meal and to be awaiting it on my own in a strange city. I felt completely in control of my life.

Someone slid into the chair beside me. 'Hi!' he said.

'Hi!' I said. He was black, West Indian most probably.

'Alone?'

I could not deny it, although at that moment, so close to the previous one which I had been savouring, I wanted to. I would have liked very much to have been able to say that I was waiting for someone. But I was not.

'You don't mind if I sit here beside you?'

'No, no.' I spoke very quickly. How could you say that you did mind? I moved my knife and fork a fraction, rearranging them, as if I was obsessed with neatness. He watched my hands.

'Where you from?'

'Glasgow.'

'Glasgow, Scotland?'

Yes, Scotland. I smiled, quickly and nervously. I *was* nervous. And my euphoria had vanished. So quickly.

He called to the waiter and ordered two beers. I felt paralysed and allowed the beer to be set in front of me although I had no intention of drinking it.

'What's your name?'

'Maggie.'

'I'm Charlie.'

He extended a broad, warm hand, and I could see no other course open except to take it. My steak came but my appetite was less keen than it had been on ordering. I was sweating slightly, and could feel the dampness under my armpits and on the palms of my hands. He watched me eat whilst he drank his beer and then ordered another. My knife slipped from my fingers and clattered between my knees to the floor.

He snapped his fingers. 'Bring the young lady a clean knife.'

The young lady was dead nervous and I felt that he was aware of it. Now I knew exactly what the trouble was but couldn't quite cope. He was coloured, that was it, and there was no running away from the fact. I wasn't colour-prejudiced, certainly not, I had several coloured friends at school, Pakistanis, Indians, Chinese, and I never could have cared less what the colour of their skin was. But what was bugging me here was that if I told him to clear off and leave me alone, which was what I wanted to do, I was afraid that *he* would think it was because of the colour of his skin. It was a kind of inverted colour-prejudice. I admitted it to myself as I fiddled about amongst my French fries. If he had been white I would have unquestionably frozen him off, but because he wasn't I sat and suffered and tried to be pol:te whilst he chatted me up. I was misleading him into thinking I didn't mind his attentions, whereas all my thoughts were focused on escape. I wanted to return to my former state of bliss, speedily. Surely that was not too much for a girl to ask, the right to sit alone unbothered? There were plenty of men on their own eating steak and no girls were pestering

100

them. I almost giggled at the idea and then almost choked and he had to slap me on the back.

'You should chew more carefully. It doesn't do to gulp steak.'

I nodded, submissively. I was tempted to push my plate away with the remains of my meal on it but that would have indicated that I was finished, and then what?

'Fancy taking in a movie?'

Hurriedly, garbling my words, I said I would have loved to have gone, but I had a date. My boyfriend would be waiting for me right now. I'd have to go. Immediately, I despised myself for having to take refuge behind the idea of a boyfriend. Why didn't I just say straight out that I didn't want to go to a movie with him, or anyone else, that I wanted to continue to walk through the streets of Toronto alone and at the end of the evening return to my hotel? I lifted my eyes to his deep black ones, tried to speak, then faltered and continued gabbling about my boyfriend Phil – that was his name – had expected me half an hour back. He'd be furious, he had no patience when it came to waiting. I got up, slopping the beer I hadn't drunk and headed towards the door. The waiter called me back: I hadn't paid. Fumbling with dollar bills, my face feeling like the setting sun, I paid my debts and sneaked a little glance back towards where Charlie was sitting. He hadn't moved. He didn't appear to be looking at me either. He was studying his glass in front of him. So, maybe in the end, I had offended him, more than if I had tried to tell him the truth. Well, if I had, it couldn't be helped, and I couldn't agree to go to the movies in order not to offend him more. I had no obligation to go to the movies just because someone asked me. Defending myself furiously inside my head, I left.

Once outside, I moved fast, weaving in and out of the crowds, and on looking back I thought I saw him. I nipped into a record shop and pushed through to the back where I stood recovering my breath, not noticing if my feet were being stood on or not. They were, frequently.

'Been running?'

I jumped. This one's skin was white; he was over six feet tall, wore frayed jeans and a headband round his forehead. He seemed to fancy himself as a Red Indian. I didn't even answer him.

I pushed my way back out through the milling customers to the street, looked right and left but saw no one waiting for me. I rejoined the stream, like a car coming in from a slipway on to a freeway.

'You seem to be in a hurry.' The voice was right at my ear. It belonged to the guy with the headband.

'Yes,' I answered in a clipped voice, 'I am.'

'Okay, I can hurry too.'

'Don't trouble yourself.'

Keeping my eyes fixed straight ahead, I walked on, but my enjoyment of the night was gone: I could no longer concentrate on the city, its beat or its people. I had one of them with me by my side, in step with me, keeping me from the pleasure of being one amongst many. I gave him no encouragement, I frowned at him and then tried to ignore him, but he didn't go away. From time to time he bumped against me, whether by design of accident I could not tell for I did not look to see, or register the contact, but walked on as though untouched, as though unaccompanied. How perverse life could be, for often when I had felt lonely no one had ever appeared to take the edge off my loneliness!

Irritated, I decided I had to try to shake him off. Abruptly, I halted, and looked into a window full of cheese-cloth shirts. Behind my reflection in the glass I saw him, his head clearly topping mine. I was tempted to stick out my tongue at him but that might have encouraged him. I maintained a stony stare.

When I continued my promenade I was heading back for the hotel, although being none too certain of the exact route I might have to pause to read street signs which would give away my uncertainty.

Suddenly, his finger gripped my elbow. 'What about a drink, eh?'

'No, thank you!' I sounded, and felt, prissy. My more natural inclination would have been to have kicked him in the shins but I didn't dare. He looked too tall and too strong.

'Ah, come on!' He did not slacken his grip. His fingers were like steel bands.

'I'm going to meet my boyfriend.'

'Oh yeah?'

Swiftly I jerked my arm from the pluck of his fingers. Then, even more swiftly, I ducked between two people in front and so gained a yard or two from him. Almost jogging – okay, Mrs Kennedy, I'm ready to get into it now – I made my way up the street weaving in and out of the crowd, excusing myself sometimes, often not, not caring, wanting only to reach the safe berth of my hotel away from men who wanted me to join them for a drink or a movie. I seemed to have deterred him this time, or left him behind, for I did not sense his shadow near me, although I did not look back to see.

The route returned to me as I retrod it. I made no serious mistakes and within twenty minutes saw the red neon sign of my hotel ahead. My breath was hectic and my body soaked as I pushed open the door.

The reception clerk gave me my key and I ascended to the quiet seclusion of my room where I flopped on to the bed. So much for being female and alone in the big city! So much for being cool, sophisticated, and worldly-wise! It hadn't lasted long. Now that the intoxication was gone

I was left with a hangover and had quite a bit of resentment about it. It didn't seem possible for me to cope with being here alone as I wanted to do: I needed help and the only help I could seek would be from Phil or Mike. That fact too I resented.

The telephone rang beside my head. I lifted the receiver and the clerk said that there was a friend below who wanted to see me. With a flood of relief I ran from the room, along the corridor, jumped into the elevator and descended, but even as the doors of the elevator were opening, I was wondering how on earth either Mike of Phil could have known where I was. And of course they could not have known.

The friend who wished to see me was the guy with the frayed jeans and the headband.

'Go away!' I said. 'Leave me alone. I'm not interested. Do you understand? *Not interested.*'

Then I stamped into the elevator and went back upstairs, fuming both at his impertinence and my incompetence. What a fool! Back in my room, I rang down to the clerk. 'If that guy comes back tell him to get lost. He's no friend of mine, do you understand?'

'Okay, Miss, if you say so.'

I locked the door and put a chair behind it. How would I ever get a wink of sleep? I had better call Phil or Mike and get them to come over and collect me. My hand went out towards the receiver, then stopped.

No, I couldn't do it. Was it pride that made me hold back? Perhaps, but not false pride I reckoned: simply the desire to see this thing through myself, not to go bleating for help at the first signs of trouble. And after all, I was not stupid, could defend myself verbally, if not too well physically, I was eighteen years old and had some money in my jeans. I did not have to whine to Mike or Phil to come running to my rescue. Think of Freya Stark! She

104

was one of my heroines, that indomitable traveller and courageous woman.

I drew the curtains, undressed and washed; then I got into bed with *The Valley of the Assassins* by Freya Stark. In this book she tells how she went alone to Luristan in Persia with a native guide who was a bit jumpy about the possibility of being killed by bandits (and who could blame him since they were around?), going, as she said, only into that part of the country where people were *less* frequently murdered. She had gone at a time when few Europeans travelled in that region. She slept in tents, on the ground, with strange men and women, her toilette often watched closely by a number of interested men. My bed was clean and white, my door locked, and no stranger, male or female, could get in. To test myself I should be sleeping in the park or on the shore of Lake Ontario with my head on the *Toronto Globe and Mail*. Well, perhaps another time. . . . Meanwhile, I could enjoy Freya Stark's discomfort in comfort. She seldom complained, made light of any trouble, even when she was ill for a week and didn't expect to recover. I must learn to complain less, to endure with less fuss. It was one of my resolutions that had constantly to be renewed. Fussing and complaining came naturally to my family.

As I read of this woman travelling alone in fierce foreign parts I felt how silly I had been to panic at being alone in Yonge Street in Toronto with a few thousand people around me. I was feeble, tame and unadventurous. Clearly, before I embarked on any field work or serious foreign travel, or camped with tribesmen, I should have to toughen myself up. Perhaps this evening was a small beginning.

I read for a while, then laid the book on the table beside the telephone. I wished it would ring. I lay and listened to the sounds in the hotel, feet moving overhead, water running, things creaking and shifting. In spite of Freya Stark's noble example in front of me, I felt alone now, but not in a joyous way, in a lonely way.

Another of the things about my family was that we had no tradition of being on our own, at any time. We were five and we lived in four small rooms. We didn't seek out privacy, having not much use for it, and would have little to do with it if we got it.

Amongst the people I'd grown up with there was little tradition for being alone, or venturing forth alone. The girls I'd gone to school with mostly lived on at home after starting work until they themselves left to get married, or more usually, they 'lived with her mother' until they found a place of their own. Some of them when they were expecting babies couldn't go to the hospital without their mothers. My friend Isobel was amongst them: married last year, expecting this, and when she had to go to the clinic her mum went too. My mother and Aunt Jessie provided the same kind of service for one another; they 'chummed' one another to hospitals, dentists, chiropodists and spiritualists. They were fond of the odd seance now and then, although I was not supposed to know they went. 'Your mother's gey sensitive,' my father had explained. 'She's afraid you might laugh at her.' Me, laugh? Well, it was possible. I was a bit taken aback though when my father told me that, both by the thought of her sitting in a room waiting for messages from the dead (which dead?) and also because she was afraid of my laughter.

Messages from the dead? I kept getting messages from my granny, I kept feeling she was still around talking to me. That was entirely different, I told the brown reflection of myself that I could see in the dressing-table mirror: they actually came out of my own mind and were the result of my having understood her so well that I could imagine what she would say in most situations.

And what would she say in this one? I fancied I heard her chuckle, deep but soft.

So we had no tradition of being on our own, but I was going to be the first in line to change all that. I was going to venture forth, I *had* ventured forth, and that meant that at times one must be lonely. One had to learn to live with it.

Now put out your light, McKinley, and go to sleep. No one is going to run off with you before morning.

And no one did. I slept well and comfortably and awoke in the morning feeling contented with myself and this little room which contained everything that I needed, for the present.

I was going to find myself a new job that day. I had every confidence in myself now that I had managed to pass the first night alone.

The sun beat fiercely on the street although it was quite early when I emerged. I set off downtown and began systematically to go in and out of restaurants and cafés to ask if they needed any help. I wasn't going to wait for announcements or notices tacked on windows. The only way you ever got anywhere, I decided, was to go right in and ask. Naturally, I didn't expect to meet with immediate success so was not depressed by the first refusals. By four o'clock in the afternoon, however, as I drank my fifth milk shake, my spirits were beginning to flag just a little. Not a lot, you understand, but definitely a bit. It was tiring for one thing, going up and down in the heat. A couple of places took a note of my hotel number in case something cropped up and one man said he might have a job clearing tables next week. That sounded fairly promising, though I did wonder how I would manage to live, especially since I would have to find a room, pay rent for it and buy food. One of the advantages of being an *au pair* was that bed and board were provided.

107

I ate early that evening, with a magazine propped up against the ketchup bottle, and kept my eyes fixed firmly upon it. It seemed one way of sending out signals to the world that I did not want to be disturbed. And it worked for no one did disturb me. I sauntered only a little while up Yonge Street before going back to the hotel. My feet were blistered and tired.

The room was cool and inviting and already beginning to feel familiar. It was mine, whether for two days or two weeks. I went to bed and continued my adventures in the wilds of Persia.

The next day was hot and very humid, and as soon as I felt the waves of warm air engulfing me in the street I decided that I would have a day off job hunting and go to the Science Centre which I had heard was very good. I spent the entire day there, absorbed by the exhibits, enjoying the cool, air-conditioned interior; I ate lunch at the cafeteria and left only as they were closing in the evening. On my way back I bought a pizza and a bottle of 'Seven Up'. A picnic in my room would save having to eat yet another hamburger or hot dog. I was beginning to think longingly that a nice plate of mince and potatoes would be a real treat.

My third evening and night in the hotel passed uneventfully. The telephone did not ring. And no one came to seek me out. As I lay there I reflected that no one in the world – no one concerned with me, that was – knew where I was at that moment.

Day four of freedom was humid again, but I resolved that I must stick it out and do a little more foot slogging in search of work. At this rate I would spend all my money on the hotel bill and return to Scotland at the end of the summer with less money than I had come over with. That would give my mother plenty to gripe about! She hadn't been able to see the sense in me chasing across the Atlantic

Ocean just to look after somebody's kids. There were plenty of good jobs going back home in Scotland, she had informed me.

That day of searching yielded less than the previous day: no one even offered to put me on a waiting list or took my phone number. Jobs, it seemed, were not there waiting to be picked up. I bought the *Globe and Mail* and studied the Situations Vacant but there was nothing to suit me.

I picnicked again that evening in the hotel room, to save money. Counting up my dollars I decided that I would have to limit myself to spending a certain amount per day. I would have to find something soon. Otherwise I knew that the only alternative would be to go back to Glasgow, and that was something I was determined not to do.

I asked the clerk at the reception desk but he could not suggest anything. He said they didn't need anyone in the hotel to make beds or sweep floors. He said the city was full of university students and high school kids looking for summer work. He was not the most cheerful or optimistic of men and reminded me in many ways of my father who found it impossible to look on the bright side. Even when he landed a good contract, he'd shake his head and say, 'Aye well, ye never ken but it might be the last job we'll ever get.'

Another day passed. And another. And another.

By the time I had been eight days at the hotel my money was running low. As were my spirits. I sat on the bed staring at the half-eaten 'submarine' (a long sandwich, so-called because of its appearance) in my hand and admitted to myself for the first time that it was not just a possibility that I would have to go home before my time was up but that it was highly probable. I couldn't go on living in a hotel room with no job. And the chances of finding one I now knew to be remote.

Chapter 7

I threw away the remains of the 'submarine' and went out.

It was dark, the lights were lit, and people were out and about. I walked downtown and went into a bookstore. I needed something light but absorbing to read, something to distract me from the thought that tomorrow, or the day after at the very latest, I must pack up and leave. I spun the revolving stand of paperbacks around watching the gaudy colours fly before my eyes.

I reached out and took one down. Ross MacDonald. He wrote detective thrillers set in California.

'I like Ross MacDonald,' said a voice behind me.

I whirled round. 'Phil,' I gasped.

'I've got a bone to pick with you, Maggie McKinley!'

I stood and stared at him, clutching the paperback against my chest. He was half smiling, and the other half of him appeared to be registering annoyance. I waited for him to take the lead.

'What the devil did you think you were playing at? Mike and I have been searching the city for you.'

'I didn't think—'

'Didn't think?' Annoyance had taken over totally now. 'You must have realised we'd be dead worried about you. Taking off just like that and leaving no forwarding address!'

110

I told him that when I'd left the Willoughbys I'd had no forwarding address. Okay, he realised that, but surely I could have given them a ring when I found somewhere? They'd nearly been out of their minds. Did he think I'd been hijacked for the white slave trade? I grinned at him. He ruffled his hair with his hand. He said he didn't think I'd be much use as a slave somehow, I was too darned headstrong. Then we both laughed.

But why hadn't I got in touch? he asked again. I had wanted to see this thing through alone, couldn't he understand that? I'd walked out on the job and so I felt it was up to me to find another and not go squealing for help to him and Mike.

'And have you found one?'

'No.'

'It isn't easy at this time of year. Anyway, where are you staying?'

I told him what I'd done since leaving Mrs Willoughby. He had called at her house to speak to me the very evening I'd left and she'd told him she had fired me. She had also informed him I was utterly irresponsible and incompetent, and that I should never have been given the care of three children.

'She's quite neurotic. I thought so the first time we went to talk to her about the job for you. I'm sorry, Maggie, that we got you involved—'

That was all right, I replied, forgiving him easily, not feeling that I had anything to forgive him for.

'Come on then, let's go get some coffee and talk over what you're going to do next. And give me that, I'll buy it for you.'

He held out his hand for the paperback book, and meekly I passed it over, following behind him to the cash desk. Then we went out and found a café where we sat facing one another across the narrow table. The evening had taken a sudden, delightful turn. That was the way I liked life to go, for the unexpected to rear its head. When I had gone out to buy that book it had been far from my mind that I would meet Phil. During the past eight days I really had been doing my best to forget his existence. Now my best didn't appear to have been up to much.

He scratched his head. Temporary jobs were very difficult to come by, there was no question about that. But I couldn't feel worried any more. Job or no job, who cared? He went off to get us more coffee and I sat back, enjoying myself, looking around the room. Over by the window sat 'Headband' with a red-haired girl. We looked straight through one another.

Phil returned with the coffee. 'I've got an idea. I've got a cousin, Pansy, she's just had twins, six weeks ago.'

Twins! Six weeks old! I wanted to groan, but didn't. But the fact that the mother was his cousin did interest me. Apparently, she also had two other children, aged three and four, so she certainly had her hands full. On top of that her husband was a representative for a chemical firm and away from home on weekdays. He toured the whole of Ontario, which is a pretty big province. Phil thought that it was very likely Pansy could be doing with some help but he wasn't sure if she would be able to afford it. And of course I couldn't afford to give my help for nothing. 'Tell you what, I'll go and have a word with her in the morning.'

And then he glanced at his watch – did he have a date with Lois? – and said that he'd have to be getting along. He'd walk me back to the hotel first though. He linked his arm companionably through mine as we sauntered through the evening crowds.

He left me at the door of the hotel, promising to come at lunch-time the next day.

I went to my room full of blissful contentment. With

the curtains open revealing a star-studded night sky between the jagged black buildings, I did a little dance, a kind of waltz, holding out my arms as if to enfold an imaginary partner. Round and round I spun until I collapsed, breathless and laughing, on to my white bed. What a variety of moods I was passing through these days! I felt like a very sensitive balance: lay one finger on me and I responded.

Tucked up in bed, I opened my new book and read until it was finished. High life and corruption in Los Angeles. I read, I knew, with an extra absorption and enjoyment, because *he* had bought the book for me, because he himself had read and liked it. When I closed it, yawning, my eyes hot with fatigue, I lay for a moment with my arms behind my head, wriggling my toes. It was just as well that I had my privacy, that I was not sharing a room with my sister Jean or a bunch of Luristanian tribesmen. Screwball! After I'd put the light out I could feel that I was still smiling. That night I dreamt a happy dream: I was having breakfast with Phil and my granny. Waking, I was less happy, inevitably, for one of my breakfast companions was a shadow who was slipping away even as I was surfacing and trying desperately not to, even as I was trying to stay down there submerged in that region where more things were possible. But the other companion was solid and would materialise, later.

And he did. He came at lunch-time, as he had promised, his dark eyes smiling, inducing in me again that melting, floating feeling. He brought good news. Pansy would love to have me. And I wanted to go without knowing any more about her, or work conditions or pay or any insignificant details like that. I wanted to go because she was Phil's cousin. It was that simple.

In a matter of minutes, I had packed up my stuff, paid my bill and left the hotel. Phil drove me out to his cousin's house which was in a new suburb on the extreme edge of Toronto. 'It's not all that convenient for the city, I'm afraid.'

The subdivision – estate I'd have called it – was almost brand-new and looked very raw, with gardens in the process of being dug over and planted. The trees around were tiny. Most of the inhabitants were young couples with young children so at least it was not like that other suburb where the Willoughbys lived. Here people walked in the streets and children played and made noise.

When we stopped outside Pansy's house two small children went careering past on three-wheeled bicycles. They were Neal and Samantha, said Phil. I gazed after them, at their whirling legs and flowing hair. They looked as if they had a great deal of energy.

Pansy opened the door with a twin on each arm. They were both crying, the twins, that was, but their mother looked as if she was close to it herself. We went inside barking our shins on a collection of toys strewn in the hallway. Pansy kept apologising for the mess, as she flicked her hair back from her face. It looked as if she hadn't been able to get around to combing her hair either that morning but it didn't matter for she was a lovely-looking girl, with the same dark eyes as Phil's.

'Sit down, sit down!' She laughed breathlessly. 'If you can find anywhere to sit, that is.'

I offered to relieve her of one baby and she passed him over into my arms. Immediately, I wondered what to do with him for the feel of my arms seemed to increase his crying, rather than lessen it. Then he was sick, right over my shoulder, down the back of my best sweater. Pansy dumped the other baby on Phil's lap and went rushing to the bathroom to fetch a cloth but I had a feeling that the smell of sour milk would linger long after she had dabbed away the stain. She herself was wearing a nylon overall

114

She said that she lived in it, found it wasn't worth wearing anything else.

I could see Phil looking at me. He was wondering if all this was wise, if I was going to cope.

'I have to be at work in half an hour,' he said. 'Will you be okay now, Maggie?' I nodded and he said that he would call me later. Then he left us.

Samantha came in screaming, blood trickling down the side of her head. Through the incoherent sobs we made out that she had fallen off her tricycle, or rather that Neal had pushed her off it. She appeared to be more indignant than hurt. Pansy looked at me helplessly. I said that if she could cope with the babies – they were more in her line than mine – I would cope with Neal and Samantha. I picked up the little girl and carried her to the bathroom where I bathed her head and told her that brothers were ghastly. They were always doing things like knocking you off tricycles but not to worry for when she grew up she would be able to get her own back. She stopped crying. Behind me stood Neal. I had not heard him come in. 'I hate you,' he said, enunciating the words extremely clearly. 'You're horrible.'

He could be right, I conceded. I couldn't help being horrible at times any more than he could. Then I took them both by the hand and asked them to show me their toys.

It was one of the most hectic, exhausting days I have ever spent. Pansy struggled to appease and feed the two babies, whilst I entertained and watched over Neal and Samantha, and tried, in between times, to clear up the chaos in the house. The chaos was indescribable so I shall pass over it quickly.

There was no rest even in the evening for the twins would not settle. Pansy thought they had wind and wondered if one of them might even be beginning to teethe. Whilst she went from one to the other I washed up the day's dishes and rinsed through some disgusting nappies that must have been soaking in a pail for some time, judging by the look and smell of them. When the telephone rang and it turned out to be Phil on the line I could scarcely carry on a conversation with him. He kept asking me stupid questions, such as did I think I was going to like it all right? Like it? It was only going to be a case of surviving. He sounded anxious, said that if it didn't work out I shouldn't feel I had to stay because Pansy was his cousin. He hadn't realised, he said, that it was such a bad scene.

'I'll call you tomorrow,' he said, and rang off, presumably to go and see Lois. My dreaminess of the night before was not going to be recaptured this evening. At eleven o'clock, after Pansy had fed the twins for the last time that day, or at least, we hoped so, we both fell into bed. I was too exhausted to think about Phil and fell asleep at once.

At around five thirty a.m., when the birds were embarking on their first chirpings outside, I was awakened by a small, flying body landing right in the middle of my stomach. I gazed into the brown, wide-awake eyes of Samantha. Laughing, she pummelled my chest with her small fists. 'Get up! Up! Up!' She kept up her pummelling and her demand until I had no option but to rise, cursing under my breath, and throw some cold water over my face. In retrospect, my stay at the Willoughbys' looked like a rest cure in a first-class hotel. But then, I reminded myself, that had been demanding and exhausting in a different way.

By nine o'clock in the morning I felt as if I had done a full day's work. I am not an early bird by nature, preferring the night-time. I could see I wouldn't get much chance here to enjoy night-time occupations and, whether I liked it or not, I was going to have to face the world early every morning. It took Pansy most of her day just to keep the babies pacified, so I was left with the other two and the house and the shopping and the cooking and the washing-up. Pansy kept saying it was terrible, I had too much to do, and she had never intended that I should do all of those things. She had thought it would be nice if I came and took Neal and Samantha for two or three hours a day, to give her a breathing space. That would have been enough, especially since she couldn't afford to pay me very much. And here she blushed a deep red. Had Phil told me what she could pay? I supposed that he had but I hadn't been listening. I didn't feel like asking her now so I just said yes, he had told me and it was okay.

'Are you sure? It doesn't seem very much for all the work you're putting in.'

I felt confident it wouldn't be enough for the amount of work I was putting in but what did it matter, as long as I had somewhere to sleep and food to eat? And as long as she gave me something that would count as pocket money. I was fast abandoning the idea that I would return rich from North America at the end of the summer. I'm sure my mother was expecting me to arrive with a sackful of dollars. She thought that everyone in Canada or the United States made 'a mint of money', as she termed it. It was as if she expected dollar pieces to be lying in the street waiting to be picked up. I could see that Pansy was having a struggle to manage financially with four small children and one salary to keep all of them, and a mortgage to pay. I was surprised that she could even afford to feed me.

I soon made the acquaintance of the rest of the neighbourhood kids. Since there were no walls or fences here between the houses the children moved freely from one garden to another. As luck would have it, most of the

117

children seemed to spend their time gravitating towards our patch of scruffy lawn. 'Hey, Maggie, give us a ride!' 'Hey, Maggie, I've cut my foot.' 'Maggie, he kicked me. He did too.' Everywhere I went I seemed to be pursued by the cry of, 'Hey, Maggie!' I was beginning to feel like the Pied Piper.

Phil called in during an evening lull when Pansy and I was sitting collapsed together in front of the television set watching a string of commercials with little bits of drama in between.

I struggled upright and managed to conquer my fatigue. Pansy disappeared to make coffee.

'How's it going then?'

Not bad, I said, I was still alive, if only just, and that I considered to be a triumph in itself. He laughed. Did I want to stick with it then? I told him I didn't think I had much option, there didn't seem to be thousands of people beating on the door to offer me cushy, well-paid jobs. Anyway, Pansy needed me; and I added cynically that it was nice to be needed. He laughed again, a trifle uncertainly, I fancied. Then I softened and said that I liked Pansy very much indeed, we were getting along just fine together.

'That's great,' he said, sitting back with relief.

Pansy came then with the coffee.

Phil dropped in most days for an hour or so, the visit usually terminating in the same fashion. He would look at his watch, gulp down the last of his coffee or coke or beer and say that he'd have to be going. To meet Lois? I presumed so. I felt myself freeze whenever he looked at his watch and always said my farewells a little coolly, in contrast to my greetings which were decidedly warmer. We spent many a good hour together, the three of us, in a cosy huddle, laughing and talking.

'He's a great guy, my cousin,' said Pansy. 'I'm real fond of him.'

'He hasn't brought Lois around for a while.' Pansy was looking thoughtful. I was glad she had brought up Lois for it gave me a chance to talk about them.

'They're still going together then?'

'Oh yes.'

'Seems pretty serious?'

Pansy considered. 'Wouldn't say that. Just going together.'

'She's a lovely-looking girl.'

'Mm.' Pansy began to lift nappies (sorry, diapers!) from the clothes horse and fold them. 'She came to see me one day. . . . Wanted to talk, about Phil, and you.'

'Me?' My heart did a loop-the-loop.

'Said things hadn't been the same between her and Phil since you came to Canada.'

'That's ridiculous.' I laughed, artificially.

'Is it?' Pansy turned her wide dark eyes on to me; it was like looking into Phil's eyes.

I had to get it all out, I'd had no one I could confide in about my feeling for Phil, and I needed to discuss my disappointment and confusion. Pansy was a good person to talk to: she listened carefully, which not everyone does, and was sympathetic without saying things to please me for the sake of it. You know how a lot of folk say what you want them to hear and that's no help at all?

'Poor Phil,' was her first comment. Poor Phil! My indignation flared briefly and died. Pansy thought it had been a very difficult situation for him; he'd been going out with Lois for a few months, liked her pretty well presumably, and couldn't just give her the go by because I was coming over for the summer. After all, we *had* only known one another for one week.

'That's true,' I sighed. 'Quite true. Lois has nothing to worry about then.'

That was where the question mark came in, said

Pansy: was Phil still attracted to me? Lois seemed to think
he was. Hope surged in me but I squashed it, as best I
could.

'Suppose he could be attracted to two girls at once,' I
said gloomily. It didn't even mean he had to be in love
with either of us, and if that was the case then I thought
Lois would have every advantage over me. This was
ridiculous, I tried to tell myself, although I knew the
information wasn't penetrating very far into my head: I
was thinking in terms of being at war with Lois for the
possession of Phil. The idea horrified me.

'I'm going to forget him,' I said.

Pansy smiled.

A sudden shriek overhead split the silence above.
Pansy sighed and got up, saying that she might have
known it would be too good to last. She went upstairs.

Not long afterwards I followed. To bed, to sleep, but
not to dream, or at least not to remember what I dreamt.
It was probably as well that I didn't for my dreams would
have been full of squalling infants. And my mornings
were so rudely shattered that I had no time to lie in bed
and ponder on Phil or my granny or anything else.

We didn't leave the subdivision, except to go to the
shopping plaza a couple of miles up the road. I stayed in
the car with the kids whilst Pansy bought the week's
groceries. Bouncing a twin on each knee, I watched the
young mothers push their trolleys in and out of the
shops. They were laden high. As I watched I knew more
than ever before that this lifestyle would never be for me.
It was all right on a temporary level, like this, but
certainly not for good. I could not live out a life narrowed
down to such a small circle; I would have to push
outward, no matter how difficult or painful it might be.

Mike came one evening, unexpectedly, unannoun-
ced, to ask me if I'd like to go out with him.

'Off you go,' said Pansy. 'You need a night out, Maggie.'

She was right: I did, and was quite pleased to see Mike. We drove off and as we left the confines of the subdivision behind I felt as if I had been incarcerated there for a decade. I told Mike so and he laughed. Where would I like to go? he asked. Downtown, I said, I wanted to walk along the streets and be trampled on by people. He laughed again. We walked up and down Yonge and Bloor Streets, stopped for a hamburger and a cup of coffee, and went in and out of the record shops. It was a good evening, and after the first few minutes' initial embarrassment, we were quite at ease. Mike was more the light-hearted boy I remembered from Scotland last year, joking, not seeming to take anything very seriously. Our moods matched.

It was midnight when he drove me back to Pansy's. Most of the houses were dark, except for the odd light shining here and there, marking no doubt a house in which a small baby was wide awake demanding attention. We sat for a few minutes in his car outside, talking.

'I'm sorry about the business in Ottawa, Maggie.'

'That's okay, Mike. You don't have to say anything more about it.' He stared ahead of him, his hands holding the wheel. 'You're pretty keen on Phil, aren't you?' he asked, and his voice sounded a trifle thick.

Keen on Phil? I began to protest. Not really. I liked him of course. I always had, but there was nothing much more to it than that. I didn't really want to get involved with any boy too much at present, I had my career ahead and so forth. I began to prattle.

'Come off it, Maggie! You're real gone on him and you know it.'

'I know nothing of the kind!'

121

'Sure you do.' Mike turned to look at me now, to search my face for some kind of truth in the semi-darkness. 'Any fool would know it.'

How could they? I demanded. He said that I had spent most of the evening talking about him.

I must go, I said, reaching for the door handle. He caught hold of my arm.

'Don't be mad at me, Maggie. But it is true, you know, you do talk about him. All the time.' I apologised, but he said that I didn't have to. He said that he understood, but he would still like to see me sometimes and take me out, if that was okay with me? It was, I said, and before I left gave him a quick kiss on the cheek.

'Thanks, Mike, you're a real pal.'

'You're welcome!'

'Is that you, Maggie?' called out Pansy as soon as I opened the front door.

I went up to her room. Had I awakened her? Of course not. She had, in fact, been pacifying Samantha who had been looking for me. 'Want Maggie,' she had been crying. 'You see what a hit you've made?' said Pansy. Then she said that I seemed to have made a hit with Mike too, that he seemed kind of keen on me. I shrugged. Wasn't I interested in him? Not particularly. I liked him, of course, thought he was a nice guy but—

'I see.' Pansy smiled and lay back against the pillows. I looked at her sharply and her smile broadened. 'How's your forgetting going?'

From the other room Samantha called out, 'Maggie!' At times children could be useful. Hastily I went to comfort her, to gather her up in my arms and tell her that it was all right, I was here.

'Whatever will we do when you leave us at the end of the summer, Maggie?' said Pansy in the morning, as she sat feeding one of the twins and I stood at the sink doing

122

the daily diaper wash. 'The kids'll miss you a lot.'

'They get used to things quickly, don't they?'

Pansy laughed, making the baby gulp. 'You like to appear tough and unsentimental, don't you?' But she spoke softly and not aggressively. As far as I could see there was not an ounce of aggression in her body, although I didn't doubt she would muster some if she had to protect her children.

At week-ends Pansy's husband Bob came home. And those were the only times when I felt a bit out of place. It was not that I didn't like him, or that he didn't like me; it was merely that I felt a bit superfluous. He tended to distract Samantha and Neal who dropped everything the moment they saw his car pull up outside. Maggie was no longer required, so at week-ends I busied myself in the house, cleaning up, even doing a bit of baking. I pored over recipes for frosted fudge cakes, lemon meringue pies and blueberry tarts.

Phil came one week-end, with Lois. Bob produced beer and Pansy put on records. I squatted in a corner feeling quiet, glancing at Lois whenever I dared. She *was* attractive, and no one, not even Pansy, could deny that. Phil, it seemed to me, was trying to avoid my eye. He was also quieter than usual.

Glancing out of the window, I saw Mike's car drawing up. I jumped to my feet. 'It's Mike,' I cried, rather too gaily. I saw Phil glance quickly at me.

We ended up by having a bit of a party and I produced my latest creation, an almond frosted fudge cake. Phil said that he had no idea I was so domesticated and I told him that that made two of us and he should take full advantage of it for it wasn't likely to happen too often again. But on the whole I gave my attention to Mike, overplaying it, talking to him vivaciously, sitting close to him. All that I only realised later, in bed, looking back on the evening, for at the time I had really very little idea of what I was doing. But lying in the darkness, watching the sliver of moon in the gap between the curtains, I knew that I had been putting on a display for Phil's benefit. I has been trying to convey the impression that I thought Mike was fantastic, that I was pretty sweet on him. What a fool I must have made of myself! My face burned. In that room several people must have known that I was not really keen on Mike at all, at least not in the way that I had been trying to imply. And foremost amongst them was Mike himself.

Chapter 8

No agonies of self-recrimination were possible the next day for Samantha was sick. I spent most of the time mopping up and comforting her. By the time I dropped into bed like a stone that evening I was too tired to think about myself.

A day or two later Phil rang up to say he had the following day off, and that he would like to take me out. I almost dropped the receiver out of my silly fingers. He wanted to take me to a place called Sainte Marie among the Hurons. It was the reconstruction of a religious community which existed between 1639 and 1649, founded and maintained by Jesuit priests from France. The settlement had been built as a retreat for weary priests as well as to show the Huron Indians the European way of life. Phil thought I'd find it interesting since it gave a picture of a way of life three hundred years back in Canada on the edge of the wilderness.

I felt like a child getting ready for a special treat. I washed my hair and pressed my jeans. Phil had not mentioned Lois and I had not asked about her.

He came early in the morning, before eight o'clock, and soon we were on our way heading out of town. Sainte Marie was about two to three hours' drive from Toronto. I sat beside Phil feeling that I must be grinning all over my face, Cheshire-cat-like.

'Lois working?' I managed to ask eventually.

'Yes,' he answered, his eyes on the road. And that was that.

A day with Phil and no Lois! It was like a gift from heaven. During the drive Phil told me about the Jesuits and the Hurons, saying he'd thought that since I was going to study social anthropology this was a place I should see. He had heard from Mike how much I had enjoyed Upper Canada Village. For a moment I felt myself sink inside: I wondered if Phil was doing this because he felt he owed me a day out, because he felt he ought to do something for me whilst I was in Canada, something to match my day with Mike. But then I pushed the thought aside, for after all what good would it do me to have it? At times negative thoughts swarm in my head like those dratted mosquitoes.

Sainte Marie had been reconstructed on the exact site of the old settlement, which the Jesuits had been forced to abandon because of their persecution by the Iroquois. Many Hurons, along with several priests, had been viciously massacred, and some tortured to death. We saw a shrine erected to the martyrs nearby.

The habitation was built within a compound, surrounded by a high wooden fence like a stockade, necessary no doubt for keeping out those marauding Iroquois. It must have been a bleak, tough life for the Frenchmen who came all the way across the ocean and up the St Lawrence River on that long rigorous journey. When they had first come they had lived with the Hurons in their longhouses, coughing on the smoke, eating the Indian food, being bitten almost to death by the insects (they had my sympathy there!) and suffering intense heat and cold. After a while they had built their own houses, some of which we could see here now.

It was quite different of course from Upper Canada

126

Village, which, in retrospect, seemed incredibly civil-ised and advanced. Of course this predated that by two hundred years, which in Canadian history is a long, long time. I was beginning to change my conception of a time scale, to bring it into line with North American history. The buildings were wooden and fairly simple. And, as in Upper Canada Village, there were people around as props, dressed as Jesuits or Indians. It certainly couldn't have been an easy life, I observed to Phil, as we surveyed a dormitory of narrow wooden beds, and he said he wouldn't have fancied it too much himself. But perhaps, on the other hand, it might have been exciting at times. He wouldn't have minded crossing the ocean and coming down the river and building the settlement. He wasn't so sure that he would fancy the life after that point, being confined within this stockade, trying to bring Christian-ity to the Hurons. 'Repelling the Iroquois could have been okay.' He grinned. 'What about you – would you have fancied that life?'

It was a difficult question, for no European woman had ever had a place here and so it was difficult to imagine what one would have done. I tried, as I went from house to house, into the cookhouse and church, and around the Indian Settlement, to put myself into the skin of a young Jesuit priest. Presumably you'd have had to burn with great conviction to endure the hardships. Phil said that as an anthropologist I might have to endure quite a lot of physical hardships, though not so severe as the Jesuits, and therefore I would have to find what I was doing so fascinating that I was prepared to put up with almost anything. I made a face. Well, I could put up with *almost* anything. As long as there weren't too many mosquitoes or blackflies around.

Inside the longhouse, made of bark and poles, there was the traditional Indian fire smoking in the middle. My eyes began to stream as we approached it. Phil told me that Indian women tended to die before their men, usually of eye and lung diseases brought on by the smoke from their fires. They spent much more time inside the longhouses than the men of course. I was kind of glad that I hadn't been an Indian woman in the seventeenth or eighteenth century. But I liked the look and feel of the longhouse, and would have liked to linger in it more, if it had not been for that infernal, catching smoke.

I found the settlement fascinating, and by the time we had gone around twice, I was forming a picture in my mind of what life would have been like for both the Jesuit and the Indians.

We left to go up the hill and have a picnic. I'd cut a big stack of sandwiches and Phil had brought fruit. From up there we could look down on the roofs and see the shape of the compound. It looked a tight and self-sufficient place and on winter evenings perhaps it had felt snug and safe but when the barbarous Iroquois hordes had arrived they wouldn't have stood much chance.

'Have a nectarine,' said Phil, putting one into my hand. My teeth sank into the fruit and juice spurted out and ran down my chin. I adored nectarines. Before this summer I had never tasted them.

Leaning on his elbow, Phil asked idly if I was enjoying Canada. Yes, I said, indeed I was. He said that of course I'd only seen a tiny fraction of it, I would have to come back and see more another time. He paused, then said, 'I liked Scotland a lot. I'm hoping to go back over next summer after I graduate.' He went on to tell me that he had applied to go to Edinburgh University to study for a Ph.D.

I would be in Edinburgh, at university next year. I did not say so, because he knew it. We lay back on the grass and looked up at the blue, almost cloudless sky. It was hot day but there was a little breeze blowing, taking the extreme edge off the heat, and from what I could tell there was almost no humidity. It was a perfect summer day, in all respects, as far as I was concerned. I closed my eyes and drifted off into a light doze.

Phil must have slept too for sometime later we woke simultaneously and turned to look at one another, rubbing our eyes and yawning. Together, we laughed. He put out his hand to me and said, 'Oh, Maggie!'

Hurriedly, I backed away, quite literally, shuffling over the ground like a crab, rubbing my right leg and saying that it had gone to sleep. It was zinging with pins and needles. Phil took hold of it and rubbed it, hard, until I had to shriek for mercy and ask him to stop. And then, afterwards, when we subsided and sat again side by side looking over the valley and at Sainte Marie, I cursed myself inwardly for my clumsiness. At that point he had turned to me, there was no question about it, and I had retreated. It had been my instinctive reaction.

Phil said that he thought we might take a run down to Wasaga Beach on Georgian Bay and go for a swim. It was a bay on the edge of Lake Huron. We ran down the hill, jumped into his car and drove to the lake.

It surprised me for it looked almost like the sea, with wide empty horizons and clean white sand along the edge. Lots of people had built cottages on the shoreline, mostly tucked in amongst the pines, not spoiling it too much. Phil told me that it was a very Canadian 'thing' to have a summer and week-end cottage, much more so than in Britain. Pretty well everyone he knew had a cottage somewhere. His family had one in the wilds of Quebec.

The water was quite warm, and there were white frothy waves to leap in and out of. Apart from the lack of salt, it was like being at the seaside. I had done very little

129

bathing outside before coming to Canada, for the sea off the coast of Scotland is not quite warm enough for my liking and I therefore had done most of my swimming in chlorinated pools. Phil wrinkled his nose and said he didn't fancy that. When he had been in Scotland with Mike he had bathed in the North Sea and the Atlantic.

'But you're tough,' I murmured, as we lay on our stomachs on the sand.

'And you are tougher than you like to make out, I'm thinking.' He ducked his head sideways to watch the reaction on my face.

I flipped a little sand in his direction. He said that when he came to Scotland he was going to drag me into the North Sea by the ankles. I could protest all I liked but he wouldn't rest until he had seen me in there, fully submerged. 'Beast,' I said, sticking out my tongue at him just a little. I was under no illusions that to stick one's tongue out fully would be at all attractive and I had no wish to appear unattractive to Phil, in spite of the fact that I had backed away from him up on the hill.

Part of me was pleased by the things he was saying, by what he was suggesting, which was, basically, that next year, when he came to Scotland, we would be together. And the other part of me was furious and resentful, thinking, how dare he think he can pick me up and set me down when it suits him! Next year, when he would be free and Lois not around (meanwhile, he could spend this summer with her), he imagined that I would be available. Neither side won the battle: they continued to wage war with one another whilst I lay on my stomach, leaning my face on my hands, staring out at the shimmering blue water. The earlier euphoria was spent. I was more confused now; the questions were swarming once more in my head. What *about* Lois? Had he had a row with her? Did she know that he was here with me today? I kept

130

quiet, being unable to bring myself to ask the questions, or perhaps not really wanting to hear the answers. Instead I asked them in my head silently, and imagined the answers. He and Lois had quarrelled (over me, naturally!), finished with one another, for good. . . .

Don't be ridiculous, McKinley! I sat up, stretching, saying that I was going back in for another swim. Without waiting or looking at him, I turned and galloped into the waves, feeling the cold sting my warm body. I plunged on relentlessly until I was waist-high in water. Only then did I look back to see that Phil had not moved.

The sun was moving across the sky, dipping slowly down over the western horizon. Its reflection ran like a streak of fire across the water. I wondered if Phil would want to drive back to Toronto for the evening, so that he could spend it with Lois.

When we were dressed, he asked if I would fancy a meal. He knew a place not far away where they served delicious steaks. It used to be an old railway depot and had been made over into a restaurant.

We drove up there and found that it was not too crowded, we could have a table by the window. The place was furnished with antiques, and whilst we waited for our order to be served we were given copies of old magazines published around the beginning of the century. I enjoyed reading the ads for corsets and patent medicines guaranteed to cure anything from boils to bronchitis.

'It's a real neat place,' I said, with a grin, looking round. Everything about the day was neat.

The steaks came served on wooden platters with baked potatoes and sour cream. They were huge, and delicious. We didn't say too much whilst we ate. It seemed that no matter how confused my emotions were there was no doubt about the state of my appetite. I had adjusted easily to North American eating habits. To finish off I had an enormous chocolate mint sundae and a cup of coffee. After which, I declared that I thought I should burst. 'That's no a very ladylike thing to be saying, Maggie,' my mother would have said reprovingly, if she could have heard me. Phil laughed and said he was delighted to hear it.

He paid the bill, I went ahead of him and stood in the roadway smelling the night air. I could detect pines. He joined me, slipping his hand into mine. 'How about a walk before we drive back?'

We sauntered along by the edge of the lake, looking out over the glimmer of water. It was a warm, balmy evening, and I could feel a tingling sensation coming from my hand holding his right up through my arm. Even the few mosquitoes there were around were not going to trouble me tonight.

Phil stopped to point something out to me, some lights somewhere. I took a deep breath and gave a long sigh, one of bliss and contentment.

'It's been a marvellous day, Phil. I really have enjoyed it. Thank you very much.'

'You're welcome! I've enjoyed it too. Oh, Maggie!' And then his arms were around me and we were kissing one another, and I recalled again the same feeling of strong attraction that had surged up between us last year in Easter Ross. My knees felt weak beneath me, ready to buckle, as if they were stuffed with straw. I clung to him, never wanting to have to let go.

He drew back a little from me and we regarded one another at arm's length in the dim light. Even though it was dim I could see that his face was slightly troubled and I knew instinctively what was wrong. Lois.

'Lois,' I said.

He sighed, said he was sorry, perhaps he shouldn't have done that. Lois had come now as a barrier between

132

us, just as last year, James Fraser had done.

He shook his head. 'Maggie, I'm sorry. I'm all mixed up. I don't know what to say.'

It was all right, I was mixed up too, I wanted to say to him, but could not put anything into words. I stood in front of him staring at his face, still trembling a little. It didn't seem to me that there was anything to talk about, there was no point in trying to have a discussion, for what was it exactly we could discuss? The problem that existed was on his side this time, not mine. My position was clear and uncomplicated.

'It was that Canadian boy that came between us,' said James, kicking at a clump of heather. 'Well it was, wasn't it?'

'In a way, I suppose—'

'Suppose? You damned well know that it was. Everything was fine between us until he turned up last summer.'

But everything couldn't have been that fine or else Phil Ross, when he did turn up, wouldn't have changed anything. I stared at James wondering if it was worth trying to explain. His face looked hard and closed against me. I knew that he was suffering, I knew that I had made him suffer. And there was nothing I could do about it.

I said no more.

Not touching now, Phil and I walked back to the car. I asked him, since I felt I had to know, if Lois knew that he was with me. He said that she did not.

'Do you think I'm just a double-crosser, Maggie?'

No, I didn't think that at all. He said that he had wanted to have a day out with me, just one. Just one! The words rang hollowly in my heart. I knew he didn't mean them to sound as callous as they came over. He didn't mean to be cruel, he had wanted to see me and I was glad

133

of that, and yet, presumably, he still wanted to see Lois as well. On the drive back I continued the dialogue with myself. Why should I expect him to break with Lois, when I was returning home in September and she would be here all winter? She was a student at Toronto University also. It didn't make sense, not for him at any rate. And I was glad that I had had this one day: I would preserve and treasure it, and relive it over and over again. Yes, I'd get good mileage out of it! That thought at least made me smile, if a trifle ruefully.

We had a puncture half-way back to Toronto. I got out of the car whilst Phil changed the wheel. I walked up and down the road staring into the dark forest beside which we had stopped. I was glad even of the puncture for it delayed the time when we must part. Phil did not sound too glad. He knelt on the road cursing because the wheel was being difficult. But when he finished he wiped his hands on a rag and whistled cheerfully as he came to join me along the road. He stared into the trees with me.

'Do you like dark primeval forests?'

'In certain moods. I wouldn't mind ploughing straight into that one and just walking and walking.'

'You're shivering. Are you cold?' He put his arm around me and hugged me to him, rubbing my bare arms. And then the same thing happened again, the same spark of electricity was struck, and once more we were kissing one another.

This time I drew back from him.

'This won't do, Phil. We have to stop it. There's Lois. And don't say sorry to me, *please*.'

He didn't say anything; we returned to the car and drove off.

Nothing else occurred to prevent us arriving back at Pansy's house. It was way past midnight, the subdivision was asleep.

'Sit a minute,' said Phil. 'Don't go yet.'

We sat and talked. About Scotland and Strathcarron and the Clearances and his great-great-grandfather and my great-great-granny. We went back over the pilgrimage that we had made up Strathcarron last year, laughing at various aspects of it, at the way I had kept falling off the bike I'd been endeavouring to ride. My sense of balance had been a shade off perfect. The bike had been Catriona's. And I had gone with James. Of course.

He fished out our food box and found some peaches and nectarines left, and so we had a little mini-picnic, sitting in his car in the middle of the night, in the middle of that dead suburban estate. It felt cosy in his car, with the rest of the world held at bay.

I took hold of his wrist to see what time it was on the luminous dial of his watch. Three o'clock! As soon as my fingers touched the warm skin of his wrist I had to remove them. 'I'd better go now,' I muttered, putting the stone of my nectarine into the garbage bag on the floor.

'Just five minutes more,' he pleaded.

I subsided again.

A car swished quietly past us, fanning us briefly with its headlights, and when it did I saw his face. I longed to put out my hand and touch the lines of it, to hold it between my hands.

'Perhaps you *had* better go now, Maggie,' he said with a sigh.

Perhaps I had. We kissed briefly, and then I opened the car door and stepped out on to the sidewalk He got out of his side and came round to join me. He walked with me up the path to the front door, waited on the step whilst I searched for the key in the depths of my bag. I found it.

'Goodnight, Phil.'

'Goodnight, Maggie.'

I went inside.

Gingerly, avoiding the stair which I knew creaked, I tiptoed upstairs, praying that none of the children would waken, not before six o'clock at least. I desperately wanted to get into bed and lie at peace so that I could think about Phil, undisturbed.

'Maggie!' I heard the thin cry even as I was opening the door of my room. 'Is that you, Maggie?'

'No,' I said firmly, and went into my room and closed the door.

Chapter 9

'You better believe it,' said Neal.

'What?' I said.

'You've not been listening.'

'Maggie bad,' said Samantha.

'Maggie is dreaming,' said their mother, with a smile, as she passed by. I threw a wet dishcloth at her but she ducked and it missed, landing on the lino with a squish. She ran laughing from the kitchen.

I took the children to the park to play on the swings. I swung myself, up and down, up and down, going high into the sky. It was an exhilarating feeling to soar up towards the white puffy clouds. And I went down the chute too, on my tummy, making Samantha laugh and clap her hands. Neal said that their mommy never went on the slide, or the swings either. Their mommy didn't have time to go on the slide and swings, I told them: she had the babies.

I bought ice-creams and we sat in a little semi-circle on the grass, licking contentedly. Each little pleasure that day seemed ten times as entrancing as it had ever been before. In the evening, when the children were in bed and asleep, mercifully all together for once, I sat by the window on the settee, with my legs curled up behind me, watching the street. Pansy teased me gently, saying that she wondered whom I could be watching for, and then as the evening slowly passed, saying that she was sure Phil would come before long. He might be on the late shift. He might, I conceded, my happiness beginning to dim. Every time the phone had trilled that day I had shouted, 'I'll get it,' and every time I'd got it it had turned out not to be him.

Pansy put on the lights and brightly suggested a glass of her home-made wine, if I thought I could bear it. Raspberry. It was delicious, I said, as I sipped it, not tasting anything.

'It's funny he hasn't come or phoned,' said Pansy. 'You didn't quarrel or anything?'

I shook my head. No, we had had a lovely day, and I went on to say but perhaps that was all it was to be, a lovely day. Thanks for the memory, and all that.

I held out my glass for another portion of the home-made brew. Perhaps the answer would be to get drunk on raspberry wine! After a couple of glasses I began to brighten up and giggle a little. Pansy said that the wine was more potent that you thought on first drinking.

'Why don't you call him?' she suggested at eleven o'clock.

That was something I couldn't do. The next move, if any, had to be up to him. The old attraction between us had flared up again yesterday, there was no question about that, but with it had come doubts also, on his part, and I suspected that by the time he woke up this morning he felt that he should resist it and be faithful to Lois. I had no way of knowing how much Lois meant to him. And neither indeed did Pansy: she was too biased to know.

At midnight we went to bed.

I hadn't expected to sleep but I did for I was worn out and had thought about him and us too intensely during the day. Now I wanted to forget.

He did not come or call the next day, or the next. I had

138

known that he would not, once he had let the first day pass. But a part of me kept hoping that he might change his mind, that it might be taking him time to come to a decision. After a week, however, I admitted to myself that he must have opted for Lois. And when Mike came that evening and took me out for a steak dinner, I steeled myself to ask after Phil.

'Oh, he's gone on a barbecue or something.'

'With Lois?' I asked in a tone of voice that suggested I would only expect that to be the way of it.

'Uhuh. Friends of hers are giving it, down at one of the small lakes. She asked me if I wanted to come but I fancied taking you out instead.'

That was nice of him, I said, I appreciated it. I wanted to squeeze his hand or touch him, but hesitated, in case it might lead to further complications.

All right, McKinley, I said to myself that night when I lay in bed, this is it; you have to forget him now. No, not forget him, that would be silly and wasteful, but get it into perspective. You had a good day together, let it go at that. You had a good year with James. No need to forget that either.

Phil came a day or two later with Lois and I was able to greet them both cheerfully. Phil was less good at meeting me, refusing to look me straight in the eye when I spoke to him. His sparkle was lacking.

Towards the end of August, Pansy, Bob and the children went to visit his mother in Manitoba for a week. Pansy asked if I would be all right staying in the house on my own? I said that it wouldn't worry me at all for there were people all around and I knew most of them by now. I would only have to holler loudly and someone would come running.

'You're sure?'

It was only as they drove off that I realised that I had

never stayed in any house alone before. Even when my mother and father had gone on their holidays to Scarborough or somewhere similar, there had always been the three of us left, Sandy and Jean and I. And in the hotel in Toronto there had been other people in other rooms. The house seemed terribly empty and quiet as I walked from room to room picking up the debris. It had been complete chaos getting them ready to go and several times Pansy had declared that this was the very last time she would go away anywhere, for the next ten years at least. The twins had chosen the wrong time to be sick and Samantha had kept undoing all the bits of packing we had just done. In the end I had removed the two older children to the garden and instructed them to play with a ball but not to move away. I made a great mistake in mentioning moving away, for of course they did just that and it took us a whole hour to track them down. We found them eventually in some other kids' back garden, soaking wet from paddling in an ornamental goldfish pond.

'You've no idea how lucky you are, Maggie,' said Pansy. 'If I were you I would keep it that way. You've got your head screwed on well enough. It's me who hasn't.'

Bob good-naturedly told her that she'd have recovered from it all by night-time and be ready to eat her words. 'That's what you think,' she flung back at him. 'It's all right for you, you're away all week. . . .' Discreetly, I removed myself, having no wish to intrude on a domestic row. It was not my scene at all.

But when they drove away they were smiling, even the twins, and Samantha and Neal waved out of the back window until the car dwindled to a mere speck at the other end of the estate.

It *was* empty and it *was* quiet. Now that they were gone I couldn't help but wish they were back again. I didn't know what to do with myself. A whole week alone? It stretched like a desert ahead. If I had been able even to look forward to visits from Phil. . . . *Forget Phil!*

The following morning I took the bus downtown and went shopping. I was going to begin on my quilt. I purchased some linen-coloured material for the backing, and for the design some smaller pieces in green, yellow, orange and red. The motif for my quilt had come to me as I rode into town on the bus looking at the trees. I was going to make the design of a maple leaf on my quilt. The linen material I would cut into squares, and in the middle of each one would sew a maple leaf of differing colours, and then at the end I would stitch the squares together and quilt them. Before coming home I had a saunter through the city, took a good look in the shop windows since that was all I could afford to do, and had a hamburger for lunch. My trip livened me up and, refreshed, I rode back to the estate clutching my parcels on my knee.

As soon as I got home I cut the large piece of material into big squares and began work. I felt just like a Canadian settler woman might have done in the mid-nineteenth century. I intended to sew every bit by hand. Sewing machines usually proved beyond me anyway. If it was electric it would run away too fast, and if it was a treadle my feet seemed to move in all the wrong ways. The sewing teacher at school had declared that I didn't concentrate enough, and that if I worked my hands a bit more and my mouth a bit less I'd get on better.

For long intervals throughout the week, sitting in the living room by the window, or on the back porch in the sun, I worked at my quilt. It would remind me of my day in Upper Canada Village with Mike, and of Pansy and her children and this sunny little house which was agreeable in so many ways but would end by stifling me if

141

I stayed too long, and it would remind me of Phil, for thoughts of him were woven into its making, virtually with every tiny (well, *almost* tiny) stitch. Thoughts of my granny and her glen were woven in also, as were thoughts of everyone who touched my life. I discovered one of the charms of such an activity: it stilled the body, occupied the hands, and left the mind free to wander. It helped to calm me down, to stabilise me. And I needed stabilising where Phil was concerned.

I thought about going up to university. Catriona had found me a little room to rent, quite cheaply, near her flat. In it I would put my books, pictures of the McKinley-Campbell clan, some of Phil's stones which I'd brought back from Ross-shire, the old broom-head I'd found in the ruins of my great-great-granny Margaret Ross's cottage, the Eskimo carving, the mocassins, pictures of places I'd visited, and my quilt. I was beginning to gather possessions, I realised, objects I cared about and wanted to keep, I Maggie McKinley, who had always declared she wanted none. It had been one of the reasons I had broken with James Fraser. He had wanted a house, possessions; I had not. So, had I changed? I nicked off the thread with my teeth, paused to admire a completed maple leaf, and pondered. Not too much, I reckoned. The possessions I would keep would be small, transportable, and could be taken from place to place, from country to country. With James it would have been a matter of *chaises longues* and antique sideboards with legs turned out to resemble lions' paws! Not for me such monstrosities. I prefer paws left to the animals.

Also, I knew, that if something, or someone beckoned, and said, 'Abandon all and come!' I would get up and go. I put aside my quilt for the moment, thus abandoning my role of Canadian settler woman, and went out to cut the grass, becoming a community-conscious suburban housewife, clucking at the weeds, waving to my neighbours and calling back, 'Hi!' to their greetings. I liked the changeover. I liked playing roles that I would never assume in real life. It was a bit like going back to one's childhood and playing at pretend games.

While I was weeding Mike came by in his car. He pulled up at the edge of the kerb and grinned at me through the open window. 'You look as if you're really into the scene.'

I informed him that one of my attributes was to be able to take on the colour of the environment, like a camouflage. He got out of the car and joined me, admiring the neatness of the garden. Every evening at sunset I watered the flowers. And that morning I had made apricot jam, I told him, managing to burn myself only very slightly and crack but one jar.

'Great stuff!' he applauded. 'Before you know it, Maggie, you'll be—'

'Never,' I cried, laying aside my trowel and standing up.

'You think you'll prefer to grub around Central Africa or Australia?'

I certainly did. I grinned at him and asked if he would like some iced lemon juice, made by my own fair hands. Such glows of satisfaction I was getting from all this jam-making and fruit-squashing and quilt-making! I might end up as a self-contented, self-satisfied placid cow. Mike laughed, saying he doubted that.

He stayed for supper and we spent a pleasant evening together watching – would you believe it? – the television and me sewing my quilt. A really cosy domestic scene.

During that week I also wrote a lot of letters. I wrote to my parents, to Jean and Sandy, Aunt Jessie, Catriona, Mrs Clark and Mr Farquharson. It seemed to be a week for catching up, for tying in the ends, for being at peace, surprisingly. It was amazing that now I was free and could go into the city I was less inclined to. It was not really that the wiles of suburbia had seduced me; it was just that I was pleased to have some time to be able to think and be alone. Also, in the writing of the letters, it gave me time to relive some of the things I had been doing this summer, to fix them more firmly into my memory. Since I had come to live here with Pansy and the children I'd often felt that things were slipping past too quickly and I wasn't even registering them. But when I started to write I discovered that I had retained more than I had expected.

But I was pleased to see Pansy and the kids when they got back. Pansy exclaimed over my rows of jam and bottles of fruit and my quilt. 'Goodness! What an industrious week you've had, Maggie! You weren't lonely?'

Not a bit. I was really pleased to be able to make the statement. I felt I'd won some kind of victory over my natural inclination to always seek out company. I'd staked out some new ground for myself. Perhaps I'd make it yet to Luristan alone with only a guide! I'd learned, too, this summer, to accept surroundings that weren't my natural habitat and get the most out of them. With clarity I knew all this. And the knowing gave me definite strength.

'Maybe I'm cut out to be a loner?'

'Doubt it somehow.' Pansy grinned. 'Who'd you talk to? Yourself?'

Yes, I did like talking to people. Pansy and I had many lengthy evening sessions together, often going to bed far too late, considering the time we had to rise.

Bob returned to work on the Monday, and the rest of us settled back into our routine.

On the Wednesday, Pansy had an appointment to

144

have her hair cut at the hairdresser's downtown, and I told her to stay and take a look at the shops. Why not even have lunch as well? I made the offer in a fit of generosity, and after she'd gone and I was struggling with the four children I regretted it slightly. More than slightly. It would have been okay if I'd had four hands. Neal and Samantha, who were accustomed to monopolising me, didn't like having to share me with the two squealing infants. When my back was turned Samantha slapped one of the babies across the face, staining it dark-red and sending him into squalls for at least half an hour. I spanked Samantha and put her into her room where she too bawled for a whole half-hour. I appealed to Neal who, at four years old, seemed almost mature, to help me, but he was in an uncooperative mood. He proceeded to fill the kitchen sink with water until it was overflowing and then sailed his boats in it. Since I was struggling with the twins I couldn't do more than yell at him to stop and at once. He paid absolutely no attention, continuing to stand on the kitchen stool and gaze ahead, his back squarely towards me.

A moment later, the stool tipped and fell, bringing Neal down with it, introducing a third shrieking member into the household. He cracked his forehead on the edge of the sink as he came down. I ran like a demented thing from one child to the other. Only one out of the four was not crying and that was because he was lying in his carrycot in the middle of the kitchen floor sucking an old dog bone. A dog bone? Where had he got that from? The dog next door must have buried it in our garden and Samantha and Neal brought it in. I snatched the bone away immediately setting the fourth member into tears also.

It was thus, far from the state of equilibrium I'd been priding myself on achieving, that Phil found me.

'Good gracious, Maggie!' He stared around the kitchen which now resembled a battlefield. 'What's been happening?'

Nothing had been happening, I snapped at him; this was just normal, routine domestic life. Why didn't he step in and take a seat? If he could find one that wasn't littered with dirty diapers or the remains of half-eaten food.

Gingerly, he came in, and sat astride a stool. His face looked horror-struck. Had I had a flood or something? I had had everything, I retorted. But now that he was here he could at least try to do something to pacify his cousin. Neal's head was coming up with a lump the size of an egg on it. Phil got a cloth, wrapped an ice cube in it and held it to the child's forehead.

'I came to talk to you,' he said, looking at me over Neal's head.

'Well, you came at the wrong time then, didn't you?' I stuck a rusk into the hand of the baby who had previously been eating the dog bone. He flung that aside, clearly preferring the bone.

'When will Pansy be coming back?'

'Not for hours and hours, I should think. Never, if she has any sense!'

Phil set to and helped me clear up the mess. He mopped up the floor, changed Neal's sopping clothes and pacified Samantha. I managed to feed and de-wind the twins and put them down for their afternoon nap. About four o'clock we sat down, exhausted, to have a drink of iced lemon juice when in came Pansy laden with parcels and looking five years younger. She had had a fantastic day and had decided that she must do this more often; it was good for her morale. She laughed. 'That is, if you can cope with it, Maggie?'

'Maggie copes beautifully,' said Phil.

I glared at him. Now that the mess was cleared up and

146

Pansy was back, I was registering his presence more fully.

'I'm going to take Maggie for a walk,' he said, holding out his hand to pull me up from the table.

We walked round the block, several times.

Phil said, 'Maggie, I've broken off with Lois.'

I felt stiff and tight-lipped. 'So?' I couldn't seem to feel anything. I had imagined this scene many times and had always seen myself in transports of delight. *Was* I perverse?

'So – well I —' We walked on. He was having difficulty in finding the words for what he wanted to say. My mind was moving though. So he had broken with Lois now, had he, and wanted to come back to me? And I was supposed to be the dummy who sat and waited for him to make up his mind? To be available when he wanted me to be? I marched on, my eyes straight ahead, not giving him any encouragement. We kept passing and repassing the same bunch of kids and I had to call hello and wave every time.

'Maggie, I broke it off with her because of you.'

Big deal! I told him that he hadn't had to. He said that he'd wanted to, that he was sorry it had taken him so long to do it but he had been confused. Surely I could understand that? I shrugged, wishing to imply that I wasn't particularly bothered whether I understood or not.

He grabbed me by the shoulders and whirled me round to face him. 'Now listen! The moment you landed in Toronto I wanted to pack it in with Lois, but how could I, just like that? It would have seemed dead mean to do it. So I did the only other thing that it seemed possible to do and that was to try to forget you. But I couldn't. I kept thinking about you, and then every time I saw you. . . .'

I was relenting, I could feel it like the way muscles slacken in heat. Now I let myself look into his face, and his eyes melted any other resistance I had left.

'You know the way you can go on for ages drifting along, not particularly happy, not knowing what to do? And then all of a sudden, you do. Well, that was how it was for me with Lois. It came to the point where I just had to tell her.'

It had been rather like that for me with James too.

'She knew anyway. She wasn't dumb. She was expecting it.'

'Was she—? Was she upset?' I felt a pang for her now.

'Not too much. I rather fancy Lois wants bigger fish to fry than me. She likes a bit of luxury, she told me that herself.'

I did not resist when Phil kissed me. My arms slid up around his neck and we clung to one another. A course of wolf whistles echoed out around us. All the kids of the neighbourhood had gathered to watch. I waved to them over Phil's shoulder.

We resumed walking, hand in hand. He said, 'The awful thing is, Maggie, that we've let most of the summer slip by. We've only got just over two weeks left before you go back to Scotland. I kept thinking it was too late for us.'

I stopped him, whirled him about to face me now. 'Too late? For us? Never!'

Chapter 10

Having expected nothing, two weeks and two days stretched ahead like infinity. They would be enough. All things are relative, Maggie, Mr Scott my English teacher used to say to me when I was having a good gripe about things that were not exactly to my liking. He liked to tell a story of a woman who lived in a single room and complained of the lack of space. Then the Good Lord – or someone acting for him – installed, one by one, in her room, a cat, a dog, a horse, an elephant, and so on. By the time he was finished she had just cause to complain, and then he began to remove them, again one by one, until she was left all alone, in her original state. How fortunate she felt then! How spacious the room was! That was how I felt about my two weeks with Phil.

Phil decided to quit his job in Toronto at the end of the week and take the last two weeks off before he began his university term. The Canadian universities go back earlier than ours, but finish the year in May. And I gave up my job with Pansy.

We drove up to Ottawa, and already I could see the changes in the trees from my last trip north. The leaves were tipped with yellow, orange and brown: the fall was on its way. And by the time it came with its full riotous glory of colour I would be back in Scotland, with our own autumn.

Mrs Ross welcomed me warmly. Dark-eyed, she looked like Phil, and Pansy. She was so glad I'd managed to make it to them in the end. I had no idea whether or not she knew what had passed in the interval. Phil had one brother, Alan, about my age: he resembled Phil too, so I took to him at once, as I did also to Mr Ross when he came home from work that evening. We sat around the table a long time having supper, drinking wine and talking and laughing. The Rosses seemed an easy-going, comfortable family, and there was little sign of any tension amongst them.

On Sunday we drove to their cabin in the wilds of Quebec. Mr Ross had a few days off. He took his car and Phil drove his own. It took us about three hours to get there, over proper tarmacadamed roads to begin with, but latterly over unmade washboard roads, which sent me bouncing up and down in my seat. I really felt as if I was going properly into the wilds for the first time in my life. Enormous pines soared above our heads and we went for miles and miles without passing a house or seeing anyone. In Scotland I had often felt that I was in remote terrain, but not as remote as this. It was the vastness of Canada that was surprising me again.

Eventually we turned off the road on to an even smaller narrow track, with trees growing high on either side, and somewhere to the right of us was a glint of water. My impression of the region was one of high pines and lakes and quietness. Phil said they loved coming up here and wherever he went in the world he would always remember this place and want to come back. He seemed to feel about it the way I felt about my granny's glen in Inverness-shire.

After about five miles on the bumpy rutted track, we saw the Rosses' cabin on our right-hand side, a simple wooden building built up on stilts looking out over the lake. The lake was incredibly beautiful, deep green and completely still, fringed with trees all around. There was only one other cabin on the lake on the far shore, although Phil's father said he wasn't too hopeful it would remain that way for much longer. Every year more and more people penetrated further into the wild parts of the country. He said it without any grudge, for, after all, he added, if he like to enjoy his country why shouldn't everyone else?

Within a day the place had put a spell upon me, caught me too with its attraction. It was like being in a green paradise: green water and green trees, tinged with the bright colours of autumn. I felt conscious of something bigger and grander than myself moving all around me; I felt myself becoming absorbed in it, and accepted the peace it offered. Yes, I, Maggie McKinley, whose mind is normally a whirlpool of activity, felt at peace.

We swam, dived, canoed, watched birds. Phil's mother, unlike Mike's and James's mothers, did not want to convert me to anything, neither to basket weaving nor jogging, to honey nor fresh air; and she was unconcerned, or seemed to be, as to whether I was in love or not with her son. She let me be, which was just what I wanted. She was involved in her own interest: she was an artist and painted all day long sitting on the deck of the cabin looking out over the water.

Phil's father fished and swam and canoed. He went out often in the boat with Alan leaving Phil and me to wander alone together through the forest paths. The smells made me feel giddy at times. I said to Phil that I could stay here for ever and he laughed, doubting me, knowing me well enough. He knew me surprisingly well. I seldom needed to explain myself to him. Okay, so maybe I couldn't spend my whole life in the wilds, but I could want them sometimes. They were the perfect antidote to the city.

City streets and wilderness. They were both for me. The parts in between I could manage without; I might stop off in them from time to time to renew friendships, or even to take a rest. I felt that my time at Pansy's had been a rest, strangely enough, even though I had been worn out physically by the children. It had been a sort of 'time out'.

In the evenings we sat on the deck watching the sun go down on the far side of the lake. We talked very little then. To chatter would have seemed brutal. The evening had a very special kind of stillness. My granny would have loved it here: it was her kind of place. She would have sat for hours watching the water and the trees and the sky. She was often in my thoughts on those quiet, languid evenings.

Mr Ross's time ran out and they had to go back to Ottawa. Mrs Ross sighed and said she wished they didn't have to leave. But they must.

'I take it you two want to stay on here and not come back to town?' she said, looking at Phil.

He looked at me. I nodded.

And so, for my last week in Canada, Phil and I were alone together in the wooden cabin beside the beautiful deep green lake, surrounded by trees and birds and animals but by no other human beings. There was a feeling of inevitability about it as I lay in his arms listening to the bull frogs croak at night, and I wondered how I had ever doubted that we would come together. I looked back on the see-saw of torment I had swung up and down on during the summer and it was as if it had all happened to someone else. And yet, every moment of that was blended into this week helping to make it what it was. I smiled into the darkness, feeling wisdom within my grasp, even for a few minutes. My life had never been so serene, so whole. And, oh, yes, I knew at the same time that the feeling would not last – could not last – but that

152

fact was of no importance whatsoever.

'I love you, Maggie,' said Phil.

'I love you, Phil,' I said, quite effortlessly. I, who had always felt the word would stick in my throat if I tried to use it. We didn't find it an easy word to say in our family and I couldn't recall ever having heard my mother or father tell me that they loved me, even though I knew that they did.

The days slipped slowly by, like beads moving on a string, each one rounded out, smooth and complete. Perfect.

I didn't think about the week ending. At the back of my mind I knew that it would, that it would have to be faced, but until it did I was going to pretend that we were living in eternity.

The morning came, inevitably.

We got up early and sat out on the deck looking at the mist hovering over the pale water. The birds that hadn't migrated were chattering in the trees, and the sun was struggling to come up.

'We'll be back here again, together,' said Phil, taking my hand. I nodded, feeling that it must be so.

We were quiet as we cleaned up the cabin and packed our things. Then, with a last look out over the lake, we got into the car and drove up the bumpy track, heading back towards civilisation.

Civilisation didn't appeal too much once we hit it. Traffic, people, noise. They were enough to make us want to turn and head once more into the wilderness, to remain there and never come out. We contemplated it, wondering how long we could last living off nuts and berries and fishing from the lake. If only it had been spring and not fall, we might have stood a chance, but with winter coming the lake would freeze and snow lie thick on the paths.

That night we spent with Phil's parents, and the following evening Phil drove me down to Toronto, on the first stage of my journey home. We were to stay that night at Pansy's, so that I could catch my flight from Toronto airport next day. The children were pleased to see us again and gave us a boisterous welcome, clambering all over me, climbing up my back with their sharp little feet. We tried to be bright, Phil and I, but my eyes kept moving to the hands of the clock. The last few hours were slipping away and could not be held back.

The day was wet, rain ran down the windows, but I was determined not to be mournful, to grumble or complain. It had been a good summer after all – what more could I expect?

I parted from Pansy and the children with promises to write and to return. The children's voices pursued us down the path into the car.

We drove to the airport and Phil waited until my flight was called. We sat in the cafeteria and drank lousy coffee out of cardboard cups and stared at one another across the table. I wanted to say all sorts of things but there was no need for them to be said, they had all been said one way or another during the last two weeks.

'Say goodbye to Mike for me.' I had just remembered him. How awful that was! And how kind he had been to me!

Phil nodded.

And then the moment came: I had to go, to kiss him goodbye, to leave him.

'I've been so happy, Phil.'

'Me too, Maggie. Me too!' He held my hands. I had to go. I went.

'See you next year, Maggie,' he called after me. 'In Scotland.' We promised one another that we would not actually say the word goodbye. As I went through the door towards the departure lounge, I looked back and waved. He waved too, our eyes engaged, and then I turned again and was out of his sight.

We flew back on a Boeing 747, which had to land at Montreal to pick up other passengers. I felt like an old hand at the flying now and did not sit full of trepidation as I had coming the other way. There were other things on my mind now anyway.

We took off on time and one hour later landed at Montreal where we sat for more than two hours, due to some breakdown in the electrical system. It was then that I felt restless and wished to be on my way; it didn't seem to be so bad when we were moving but whilst we were sitting on the ground I kept thinking that I could get out of the plane and jump into a taxi and go back to Phil. From Montreal it wouldn't be all that far to the Rosses' cabin in Quebec. It seemed crazy for me to be leaving him when we had been so happy together, and I wasn't going to see him again for at least nine months. That stretched in front of me like something worse than eternity.

Fasten your seat belts, ready for take off. . . . We took off again smoothly, and I let out my breath with relief when we were up. That part especially still seemed miraculous to me. The stewardesses came round again with their drink trolleys. We were crossing over Newfoundland and very soon were over the Atlantic Ocean, so the captain told us. When I knew we had left the shores of Canada behind I felt a bit better. It was irreversible now, our parting; it must be faced and accepted.

We had made no promises to one another, Phil and I, we had not felt them to be necessary. This was one of the aspects I valued about our relationship. He did not talk to me about things like engagements or marriage, he did not want to press me into full-scale commitment. I did not want it, at least not yet. Each step of my life I must take as it came, and that was something James had not understood. I hadn't wanted to pledge my entire life away to him whereas I would have been content to have gone on as we were at that time. And so now it was with Phil, only I felt more in harmony with him than I had with James. Anyway, I believed that that was so, in so far as I could determine it. The exact truth was difficult to know, for often, when one thought about a problem or situation, it seemed to appear in a different light at different times. It was possible to convince oneself of almost anything, I decided, given the right motivation.

Phil would come to Edinburgh next summer but I was not going to spend the months between pining and moping. That would be a waste of my year at university. It didn't mean on the other hand that I was going to rush out with dozens of other boys, but I was going to go out and join in activities that interested me. There was no question about that in my mind. I had mumped and moped last winter through, in that awful binding factory. But this year would be different for I was going to be doing something interesting, something I wanted to do.

And now as Canada, and my summer, were falling away behind me, my mind was beginning to edge over towards Scotland, and the people waiting there for me, and the year ahead. The changeover was gradual and not complete, for all the time I was thinking of the other end, and arrival, I was remembering Phil, remembering his face and his voice, and thinking that he would cross the Atlantic and be with me again, thus bringing the two sides of my life together.

It was time to eat now. I pulled the little flap down from the seat in front of me and accepted my tray. Whilst I had been away I had put some meat on my bones, which my granny would certainly have approved of.

Now I thought of my granny, and realised that I had

accepted her death. The pain was still there but more muted, less sharp; it didn't twist and turn in me like a knife any longer. I knew that the cycle of life and death was inevitable, always had known it of course, but knowing is one thing and accepting another, especially when it comes home in a personal way. 'Ye canne go on forever, thank God!' I had once heard her say, and again, 'Enough's as good as a feast.' Her life had been a feast in its own quiet way. Others might not have agreed, thinking that her life had been hard and frugal and limited, but I had known her and seen the richness of it. And I was glad of that. I touched the Cairngorm brooch on my shirt. Wherever I went in the world I would carry that with me. And I would carry her with me too in a way. I would always be able to still my mind and ask myself, what would she say now? And as long as I could do that then I would not have lost her.

Perhaps one never did lose anything totally. Perhaps I had not lost all that had passed in the year that I had spent with James Fraser. I might have retained things which were woven into what I was now, and had even influenced my relationship with Phil. It was a comforting thought. And so as we passed high up over the Atlantic, heading back towards the Scottish coast, I was much less sad than I'd expected to be on this flight.

Now I thought of my mother and father, of Sandy and Jean, of Aunt Jessie and Uncle Tam. My mother and aunt would be in a tizzy, fussing around one another, unwinding the rollers from their hair, a little nervous about my homecoming. My mother would be saying she would be glad when that plane landed and she had me back safe and sound on Scottish soil. And Aunt Jessie would be doing her best to comfort her. My dad wouldn't be saying too much at all, he'd be stomping around looking for his cuff-links and demanding to know where my mother had hidden them. I grinned. Yes, going home was nice too, as well as going away.

I slept for a while.

Fasten your seat belts, make sure that your seats are in the upright position. We would be preparing to land shortly, at Prestwick.

Obediently, I fastened.

We were losing height. I was not in a window seat so didn't see the ground as we approached. And then we were going down, the wheels were in contact with the land. My own land! My heart lifted.

I could hardly wait to get out of the machine now, the delay seemed endless as everyone fussed and gathered up possessions and waited to be released. I wanted to jump out of the window, and run and find my dad who would be standing, feet planted solidly apart, at the other side of the barrier in his best navy-blue suit.

He was there all right, and so was my Uncle Tam, his red rosy face shining, and there too were my mother, looking not long out of the hairdresser's, and beside her, Aunt Jessie, her hair aflame with newly applied henna.

'We couldne wait, hen, for you to get to Glasgow,' said my mother, clutching me against her Crimplene bosom. 'We had to come.'

I hugged and kissed them all in turn, and then did the rounds again, making my mother laugh and gasp. We were not used to too many demonstrations of affection in our family. But even my father kissed me back that day. My mother kept asking me if I was all right, and I kept telling her, 'Of course, of course!' I wanted to join hands with them and dance in a ring.

'You look real great, Maggie,' said Aunt Jessie. 'More grown-up like. And you've got a smashing tan on you.'

'You should see my back!'

'Not here though,' said my father, alarmed.

158

Uncle Tam winked at me.

'Well, and how was Canada then?' demanded Aunt Jessie.

'Real neat.'

'Neat?' My mother's face puckered with non-comprehension.

I laughed. I had so much to tell them I didn't know where to begin. There was a lot I wouldn't tell them too of course. But then how could one ever tell anyone everything? They would want to know what people were eating and wearing and what they had in their houses and how much money they earned. It would take hours and hours to tell all that they would want to know.

'Come on,' I said. 'Let's get home.'

My mother linked her arm through mine, and the men led the way to the car park carrying my suitcases and bundles, my father grumbling about the rubbish I brought back with me from everywhere. I was like a tinker! There were valuable things inside that rubbish, I informed him, and he sniffed. Gold bars, prophesied Uncle Tam, from the weight of them.

Aunt Jessie's ankle wobbled. She always wore heels higher than she could cope with.

'Lean on me, Aunt Jessie,' I said, angling out my elbow for her to take.

'Thanks, hen. It's great to have someone young and strong to lean on.'

'You're welcome,' said I.

JOAN LINGARD

If you enjoyed this book, perhaps you ought to try some more of our Joan Lingard titles. They are available in bookshops or they can be ordered directly from us. Just complete the form below and enclose the right amount of money and the books will be sent to you at home.

☐ Maggie 1: The Clearance	£1.95
☐ Maggie 2: The Resettling	£1.95
☐ Maggie 3: The Pilgrimage	£1.95
☐ Maggie 4: The Reunion	£1.95
☐ The File on Fraulein Berg	£1.50
☐ The Winter Visitor	£1.25
☐ Strangers in the House	£1.95
☐ The Gooseberry	£1.95

If you would like to order books, please send this form, and the money due to:

ARROW BOOKS, BOOKSERVICE BY POST, PO BOX 29, DOUGLAS, ISLE OF MAN, BRITISH ISLES. Please enclose a cheque or postal order made out to Arrow Books Ltd for the amount due including 30p per book for postage and packing both for orders within the UK and for overseas orders.

NAME ....

ADDRESS ....

....

Please print clearly.